February 11, 2018

Dear Nelum

Congratulations on making
your first Holy Communion!
This book of Bible stories is
adapted by a famous author. I
hope you'll find it interesting. ☺

You'll be in my prayers.

Amy

The Random House Book of
BIBLE STORIES

MARY POPE OSBORNE
and NATALIE POPE BOYCE

The
Random House
Book of
BIBLE
STORIES

illustrated by
MICHAEL WELPLY

RANDOM HOUSE NEW YORK

*For our mother, Barnette Dickens Pope,
and in memory of her mother, Bertha Dickens.
Very special thanks to the
Rev. Mark H. Hatch, BA, MA, MDiv,
for his invaluable help with this book.*
—M.P.O. and N.P.B.

*For Gail, Oakleigh and Ed, Roscoe, Yuko and Hermes,
who make it all worthwhile.*
—M.W.

Text copyright © 2009 by Mary Pope Osborne and Natalie Pope Boyce
Interior illustrations copyright © 2009 by Michael Welply
Jacket art copyright © 2015 by Tim Jessell

Published in the United States by Random House Children's Books,
a division of Random House LLC, a Penguin Random House Company, New York.

Random House and colophon are registered trademarks of Random House LLC.

Visit us on the Web!
randomhousekids.com

Educators and librarians, for a variety of teaching tools, visit us at RHTeachersLibrarians.com

Library of Congress Cataloging-in-Publication Data
Osborne, Mary Pope.
The Random House book of Bible stories / by Mary Pope Osborne and Natalie Pope Boyce ;
illustrated by Michael Welply. — 1st ed.
p.   cm.
ISBN 978-0-375-82281-0 (trade) — ISBN 978-0-375-97425-0 (lib. bdg.)
1. Bible stories—English. I. Boyce, Natalie Pope. II. Welply, Michael.
III. Title. IV. Title: Book of Bible stories.
BS551.3.O83   2009   220.9'505—dc22   2007047308

MANUFACTURED IN CHINA

14 13 12 11 10 9 8 7 6 5

First Edition

Contents

The Random House Book of
BIBLE STORIES

The Creation of the World
(Genesis 1–2)

n the beginning, God created heaven and earth. The earth was without shape, and darkness covered the deep. The spirit of God moved upon the face of the waters like a wind.

On the first day, God said, "Let there be light." And there was light. God then divided the light from the darkness, and he called the light Day and the darkness Night, and it was good.

On the second day, God created the sky and separated it from the waters. God called the sky Heaven, and there was morning and evening.

On the third day, God gathered the waters together and separated them from dry land. The land he called Earth and the waters he called Seas, and then God said, "Let the earth put forth plants yielding seeds and fruit trees bearing fruit." And it was so.

On the fourth day, God made two great lights to shine in heaven. He made the sun to rule the day and the moon to rule the night. God also made stars and put all these things in the heavens to give light upon the earth.

On the fifth day, God created birds to fly across the sky, and he created great whales and fish to swim in the seas. He blessed them all and said, "Multiply and fill the skies and seas with living creatures."

On the sixth day, God created the cattle that graze in the fields and all the wild animals and everything that creeps across the earth. Then God created the first humans in his own image. "I have given you plants and trees and every animal and creature that lives. Be fruitful and multiply."

God looked over everything he had made and saw that it was good. God then blessed the seventh day and made it holy. And finally, on this day, he rested.

Adam and Eve

(Genesis 2–3)

There was no one to care for the earth, so God created a man from the dust of the ground. God breathed a breath of life into the man, and he became a living being. His name was Adam.

God created a wondrous garden to the east in a place called Eden. God put Adam in the garden to care for it. A river ran through Eden, bringing water for the plants and trees, which were heavy with fruit. But in the middle of the garden stood a tree unlike all the others. It was the Tree of the Knowledge of Good and Evil.

"You can eat the fruit from every tree," God warned Adam, "but if you eat from the Tree of the Knowledge of Good and Evil, you will die."

Then God brought all the animals to Adam so that he could name them. Adam gave names to all the tame and wild animals and to all the birds that flew in the sky.

God saw that Adam was alone. "I will make a helper for him," he said. God put Adam into a deep sleep. As he slept, God took one of Adam's ribs and formed it into a woman. The woman's name was Eve, and God brought her to Adam.

Adam and Eve lived peaceful lives in Eden. They had never known sin or evil. Often, on cool evenings, they walked and talked with God.

One day everything changed. As Eve was walking alone, she came upon an evil serpent. The serpent came from a tree and approached her. "Can you eat from any tree in the garden?" he hissed.

Eve told the serpent that they could eat from any tree but one. "If we eat from this tree or even touch it," she said, "God says we will die."

"You will not die," said the serpent. "God fears that if you eat this fruit, you will become like him. He does not want you to be as wise as he."

The serpent's words tempted Eve so much that she took the fruit and bit into it. Then she found Adam and gave him the fruit to eat as well.

For the first time, Adam and Eve felt fear and shame. Aware of their nakedness, they gathered fig leaves and wove them together for clothes. When they heard God walking in the garden, they were afraid and they hid.

"Adam, where are you?" God called.

"Lord, I heard your voice.

But I was afraid, so I hid," Adam answered.

"Have you eaten fruit from the forbidden tree?" God asked.

"Eve gave me the fruit and I ate it," said Adam.

"Why did you disobey me?" God asked Eve.

"The serpent tempted me to eat the fruit," she replied.

God turned angrily to the serpent. "Cursed are you above all animals and wild creatures on earth," he said. "From now on and forever, you shall crawl on your belly and eat dust!"

Then God spoke to Adam and Eve: "Because you have disobeyed me, you must work hard all the days of your life. You will earn your bread by the sweat of your brow. You are dust, and to dust you shall return."

God drove Adam and Eve out of the Garden of Eden. He placed an angel with a flaming sword at the entrance to keep them out forever.

Cain and Abel
(Genesis 4)

Though God had punished Adam and Eve, he still loved them. Soon they had a baby boy, whom they named Cain. A few years later, God sent Adam and Eve a second son, whom they called Abel. When they were older, Cain worked in the fields, growing food for the family, while Abel tended sheep.

Adam and Eve and their two sons often presented gifts to God to honor him. They built altars of stone, and on top of the altars they burned special offerings.

One day Cain and Abel brought gifts to the altar. Cain brought fruit, while Abel offered a fat lamb. God was pleased with Abel's gift, but not with Cain's. Cain grew angry and felt jealous of Abel.

"Why do you look so angry, Cain?" God asked. "If you try to do well, I will accept you. When you do not try to do well, evil lurks at the door."

Cain could not overcome his jealousy. "Let us go out to the fields," he said to his brother. When they got to the fields, Cain turned on his brother and murdered him.

God then called out, "Cain, where is Abel, your brother?"

"I do not know," Cain lied. "Am I my brother's keeper?"

"What have you done?" God said. "Your brother's blood is on the ground. And now you are cursed from the ground. When you till the soil, it will yield no food. You shall have no home for the rest of your life. You will live all your life as an outcast who wanders the earth."

"My punishment is greater than I can bear!" cried Cain. "Your face will be hidden from me. Whoever finds me will kill me!"

God was merciful. He put a special mark on Cain to protect him. Then Cain went away from the presence of God to the land of Nod, east of Eden.

ℕoah and the 𝒜rk

(Genesis 6–9)

s time passed, more people were born into the world. Gradually they began to turn away from God. They became so violent and wicked that God regretted his creation.

"I wish to destroy the creatures on the face of the earth," God said, "man and beast, creeping things, and birds of the air."

Only one man found favor in God's eyes. His name was Noah. When others turned away from God, Noah remained faithful. He lived peacefully with his family and served God with all his heart.

One day God spoke to Noah and said, "I am going to destroy all the evil on earth. I will send a great flood that will cover the whole world and wash away all the evil."

God then commanded Noah to build a large boat of cypress wood forty-five feet wide and four hundred and fifty feet long. The boat was called an ark. God told Noah to bring every kind of food and two of every kind of bird and beast onto the ark. All these creatures would live with Noah and his family on the ark until it was safe to return to land.

Noah and his sons got to work at once. They cut cypress wood and hammered it together. Then they waterproofed the wood by sealing it with tar.

When the ark was ready, Noah rounded up the animals and birds. Two by two, the animals walked up the ramp to the boat. Then Noah and his family climbed aboard.

"In seven days, I will send rain," said God. "It will rain for forty days and forty nights. Every living thing will be blotted out from the face of the earth."

God closed the door of the ark, and soon Noah and his family could hear the sound of rain on the roof. It rained for forty days and nights. It rained as it had never rained before. The waters rose higher and higher, until they covered the earth.

The waters rose above the tallest mountains, drowning all creeping, flying, and swimming creatures. Every living thing on earth died, except the people and animals on Noah's ark. As the sturdy ark bobbed on the high waves, the mightiest flood could not sink it.

But God did not forget Noah and all who were with him. God sent a huge wind blowing over the earth, and slowly the waters began to subside. The fountains of the deep and the windows of heaven finally closed, and the rains stopped.

At last the tops of mountains began to peep through the waters, and the ark came to rest upon the mountains of Ararat.

Noah wanted proof that the floodwaters had gone down all over the earth, so he opened a window and sent forth a raven. The raven flew back and forth across the sky, without landing.

Next Noah sent forth a dove. When the dove also returned, Noah knew it was still not safe to leave the ark. He waited another seven days and sent the dove out again. This time the dove flew back with a freshly plucked olive leaf in its mouth. Noah knew the waters

had gone down. Seven days later, he sent the dove out again. This time the bird did not return, and Noah knew it was finally safe to leave the ark.

God blessed Noah and his family and made a promise to them. "Never again will all living things be destroyed by floodwaters," God said. "The sign of this promise will be a rainbow. When you see a rainbow shining through the clouds, you will know that I shall never again destroy every living thing on earth. And when I look down and see the rainbow, I will remember my promise to you."

As Noah and his family and all the animals left the ark, a rainbow shone through the clouds and gave them comfort and hope.

The Tower of Babel

(Genesis 10–11)

After the time of the flood, Noah's children began to have children. Over time, many people lived on earth.

One day Noah's descendants decided to build a tower that would reach to the heavens. "Our tower will make us powerful and draw us all together," they said, "so we can never be scattered across the earth."

The builders set to work making thousands of bricks. They heated them well to give them strength. Then they made mortar out of tar to hold the bricks together.

At this time on earth, everyone spoke the same language. Since all the builders understood one another, their work went smoothly, and soon the mighty tower began to rise into the sky. Its great height made the people feel powerful and proud.

When the tower was at its tallest, God visited the city. What he saw did not please him. God thought that building the tower had made everyone too proud. People now believed that there was nothing they could not do. They thought everything was within their reach.

God wanted to teach the people a lesson, so he made everyone start babbling in different and confusing languages. The tower builders could no longer understand one another, so they were forced to stop their work.

People then separated into groups, each speaking a different language. The groups scattered over the face of the earth, and many nations rose up where once there had been only one.

The Call of Abram
(Genesis 12–13, 15)

good man named Abram once lived in a place called Haran. For many years Abram had been happily married to a woman named Sarai. Their only sadness was that they had no children.

One day God spoke to Abram: "You and all your family have my blessing. Your people will someday become a great nation. Go now to the land where I direct you."

Abram and his large family packed their belongings and took down their tents. They gathered their flocks of goats and sheep and herds of cattle. Then they headed south toward the land of Canaan.

Troubles began for Abram soon after he entered Canaan. There was not enough grass for all the livestock belonging to his family, and servants began quarreling over whose animals should get the most food and the best grazing lands.

But Abram was a generous man. He allowed his nephew Lot to choose the best land for himself. Lot chose Sodom on the Plain of Jordan, where the land was lush and green.

Abram and his wife stayed in Canaan. One day God appeared

before him and said, "Look north, south, east, and west. I will give you and your descendants all of this land."

Abram was puzzled. How could he have descendants when he had no children? he wondered.

"Do you see the night sky?" God asked. "I will give you a son and as many descendants as there are stars in the sky."

Then God told Abram to prepare a sacrifice. Following God's orders, Abram killed a cow, a goat, a ram, a turtledove, and a pigeon. He cut all the animals in half, except the birds, and he placed them on the altar. For the rest of the day, Abram fended off the birds of prey that circled above the dead animals.

Before night came, Abram was exhausted and fell into a deep sleep. As he slept, a terrible darkness descended upon him. The voice of God came out of the darkness. "Know that you and all your descendants will travel in lands you do not own. For four hundred years, your people will suffer at the hands of others. The people in these lands will be cruel and make slaves of your people. But then your descendants will leave and return to their own land. They will be prosperous and take their wealth with them. You yourself will live to be a very old man, and you will die in peace."

When night fell, Abram saw an amazing sight. Out of the darkness emerged a torch of fire and a smoking fire pot. As Abram watched, the torch began to move. It slowly passed over and around the sacrificial animals on the altar.

Three Strangers

(Genesis 16–18, 21)

n spite of God's promise, Abram and his wife, Sarai, remained childless. As Sarai grew older, she became convinced that she would never have a child. Reluctantly she urged Abram to have a child with Hagar, her Egyptian servant. Abram did as Sarai asked. But trouble began when Hagar became pregnant. She began to treat Sarai with contempt and scorn.

When Sarai complained to Abram, he said, "Hagar is under your control. You may do with her as you please."

Sarai's punishment of Hagar was so harsh that Hagar ran away from Abram's house. As she rested by a spring, she heard the voice of God: "Hagar, servant of Sarai, where have you come from and where are you going?"

Hagar explained that she was running away from Sarai's wrath.

"Return to Sarai," God said, "do what she wants, and I will give you descendants too numerous to count."

Hagar returned to Abram's house, and soon after, she gave birth to a son for Abram. She named the boy Ishmael, which means "God hears."

Abram was eighty-six when Ishmael was born. When Abram was ninety-nine, he still had not had a child with Sarai, but God reassured him that his promise would soon come true.

"You shall be the father of many nations," God told Abram. "No longer will your name be Abram. From now on, your name will be Abraham. You and your descendants will have all the land of Canaan. As for Ishmael, I will bless him and he will be the father of twelve princes and of a great nation. Sarai will now be called Sarah. In a year, she will have a son, and you will call him Isaac."

Shortly thereafter, God sent another sign to Abraham. When Abraham was sitting in front of his tent in the heat of the day, he saw three strangers walking down the dusty road. Abraham rushed forward to greet them.

"Come in, my friends," Abraham said. "Let us bring water to wash your tired feet. Please rest under the tree while we prepare some food."

Abraham hurried to the tent and asked Sarah to make some bread. Then he told his servants to prepare a calf for a meal. Abraham also served curds and milk to his guests. Standing under a tree, he waited patiently while they ate.

"Where is your wife?" one of them asked.

Abraham explained that Sarah was inside the tent.

"She will soon have a son," one of the strangers said. Abraham realized the stranger was God himself!

Sarah was eavesdropping from inside the tent. When she heard God's prediction, she began to laugh. She didn't believe that a woman of her age could have a child.

"Why is Sarah laughing?" God asked Abraham. "Is there anything too wonderful for me to do?"

Sarah was worried that God had heard her laughing. "But I did not laugh!" she protested.

"That is not true," God said, "for I heard you laugh."

God kept his promise to Abraham. Soon Sarah gave birth to a beautiful boy. Abraham named the baby Isaac, which means "laughter," because God had made Sarah laugh.

The Destruction of Sodom

(Genesis 18–19)

hen the men left Abraham's tent, he walked along with them for a while. They saw the town of Sodom in the distance. God told Abraham that Sodom was filled with wicked people, and he would soon destroy them.

Abraham was afraid for his nephew Lot, who lived in Sodom. "Will you destroy the good people with the wicked?" he asked God. "Suppose there are fifty good people who are in the city? As judge over all the earth, are you not supposed to be just?"

"If fifty righteous people can be found, I will not destroy the city," God said.

Abraham was still worried. "I know I am only dust and ashes," he said. "But what if there are forty-five good people there?"

Once more God relented and promised not to destroy the city with forty-five innocent people in it.

"I know that you might be angry, so I will only ask these few times," Abraham said. "But what if there are thirty good people, or twenty, or even ten good people in the city?"

"For the sake of ten, I will not destroy the city," God promised.

Then Abraham and God parted company.

Later that evening, two angels walked up to Sodom. Abraham's nephew Lot was sitting by the city gates. When he saw the strangers, Lot stood and bowed down to the ground in greeting.

"Come this way to my house," said Lot. "You can wash your feet and spend the night. Then you can get up early and go on your way."

The two angels told Lot they would sleep in the square, but he insisted they come with him to his house. There Lot prepared a feast for them and they ate.

After dinner Lot and his guests heard shouting in the streets. The men of Sodom had surrounded the house. They demanded Lot bring out the strangers so that they could harm them.

Lot went outside, closing the door behind him. "I beg you, my brothers, do not act so wickedly," he said. "I cannot send out guests who have taken shelter in my house."

The crowd grew angry and pushed Lot aside. They began beating on the door, trying to break it down. Quickly the angels pulled Lot back into his house. As shouts of rage grew louder, the two angels blinded everyone in the crowd.

Then the angels turned to Lot. "Are any of your family here?" they said. "Get them out! God will destroy this city!"

Lot dashed through the city and found the young men who were planning to marry his daughters. "Hurry! Make haste!" he cried. "God is about to destroy Sodom!" But the young men did not believe Lot, and they refused to leave the city.

As morning dawned, Lot woke his wife and daughters. They dressed quickly and dashed out of the city gates.

"Run for your lives! Do not look back or stop anywhere in the valley!" the angels urged. "Hurry to the hills, or you will die!"

As Lot and his family fled from the city, fire and sulfur rained from the heavens. God destroyed everything in Sodom . . . the buildings, and all the people.

Lot's wife did not obey the angels. She turned around and gave one last look at the burning city. In an instant, she was turned into a pillar of salt.

The next morning, Abraham looked out toward the city and the valley. There in the distance, all he saw was smoke rising from the place where Sodom had once stood.

Ishmael and Isaac

(Genesis 21)

hen Sarah's son, Isaac, grew older, Sarah did not want his half brother, Ishmael, to share his inheritance. "You must send Hagar and her son away," she told Abraham. "Isaac and Ishmael should not grow up together as equals."

Abraham was distressed, for he loved Ishmael as much as he loved Isaac.

"Do not be unhappy," God comforted Abraham. "Do what Sarah asks, and someday I will give Ishmael many descendants, and they, too, will become a great nation."

Abraham rose early the next morning. He gave bread and water to Hagar; then he sent her and her son away toward Beer-sheba.

Hagar and Ishmael wandered into the wilderness alone. When they had drunk all their water and were thirsty, Hagar sat down in despair and closed her eyes. Ishmael began to weep.

God heard the boy crying, and he spoke to Hagar: "What troubles you, Hagar? Do not be afraid. Stand up and take Ishmael by the hand and walk. I will take good care of him, give him descendants great in number, and make a great nation of him."

When God opened Hagar's eyes, she was amazed to see a well nearby. She filled her water container and gave Ishmael a long drink. Then they gathered their strength and went on their way.

From that time on, God cared for Ishmael during his days in the wilderness. As he grew up, the first son of Abraham became an expert with the bow and arrow, and when he was older, he married a woman from the land of Egypt.

The Sacrifice of Isaac

(Genesis 22)

One day God decided to test Abraham.

"Take your son Isaac and go to the land of Moriah," God said to Abraham. "There you must sacrifice the boy to me on one of the mountains."

Abraham loved his son dearly, but he wanted to obey God. With a heavy heart, he rose early in the morning, saddled his donkey, and called Isaac to him. Then Abraham ordered two of his servants to bring wood for a burnt offering. For three days father and son journeyed toward Moriah.

When Abraham saw the place in the distance, he told his servants to wait. "Stay here with the donkey," he ordered. "My son and I will go ahead and worship God. Then we will come back to you."

As Isaac and Abraham started walking toward the mountain, Isaac was puzzled. "Father, we have fire and wood, but where is the lamb for a burnt offering?"

"God will provide the lamb for the offering, my son," said Abraham.

Soon Abraham and Isaac came to the place for the sacrifice. God commanded Abraham to build an altar and place wood on top of it. Then Abraham tied Isaac up and lifted him onto the altar. Slowly he took out a knife and lifted it into the air. Just as Abraham was about to slay his beloved son, God called out to him, "Abraham! Abraham!"

"Here I am," answered Abraham.

"Do not lay your hand on the boy!" said an angel of the Lord. "Because you are willing to sacrifice your beloved son, I know you fear God and you will obey his commands."

At that moment, Abraham saw a ram caught by his horns in a thicket. He slew the ram instead of his son Isaac, and he gave the animal to God as an offering.

The angel of the Lord spoke to Abraham a second time: "Abraham, since you were going to obey me, I will bless you. Your descendants will be as many as the stars of heaven and as the grains of sand on the shore, and they will all be blessed. All the nations of the earth will be blessed because you obeyed my voice."

Rebekah at the Well

(Genesis 23–24)

braham's wife, Sarah, lived a long life. When she died at a great age, Abraham knew that he was very old as well. He called for his most trusted servant.

"You must promise that you will not allow my son Isaac to marry a woman from the land of Canaan," Abraham said. "Promise me that you will go to the birthplace of my ancestors and find a wife for him there."

The good servant promised to follow Abraham's wishes. Abraham gave the servant many special gifts to take with him. The man packed the gifts on ten camels and traveled to the land of Aram-naharaim, until finally he came to the city of Nahor.

As dusk was falling, the servant made his camels kneel down for the night. Nearby, women from the town were drawing water from a well.

"Dear God," the servant prayed, "help me find a wife for the son of Abraham. Please give me a sign. Let the girl who gives me and my camels a drink of water be the one I should choose for Isaac."

Before the servant had finished praying, a lovely girl named

Rebekah came to the well. She began filling a jar with water. As the girl turned to leave, Abraham's servant ran up to her and asked for a drink.

"Here, my lord," said Rebekah, and she gave him water. When the servant had finished drinking, Rebekah offered to get water for his camels. The servant gazed at her in silence, wondering if God was truly answering his prayer.

By the time his camels had finished drinking, the servant knew in his heart that Rebekah was the wife God wanted for Isaac. He gave her gifts of a gold nose ring and two heavy bracelets. "Whose daughter are you?" he asked. "Is there room in your father's house for us to stay?"

Rebekah assured the servant that he would be welcome at her house. "We have straw and fodder for your camels," she promised. The man then bowed his head and thanked God for leading him to Rebekah.

Rebekah hurried home to prepare for the visitors. When her brother Laban saw the gifts that Abraham's servant had given her, he rushed forward to greet the visitor. He then led the servant into his house and prepared a meal for him.

"I cannot eat before I tell you why I am here," the man said. He explained that he had come from Abraham, who was blessed by God with riches and greatness. He said that his master had sent him to his homeland to find a wife for his son, and Rebekah was the girl whom God had chosen.

Realizing the servant was doing God's will, Laban gave permission for Rebekah to go to Isaac. The servant praised God and gave the rest of the gifts to Rebekah and her family.

Early the next morning, Rebekah's mother and brother begged the servant to allow her to stay with them for ten more days. But the man replied that he could not delay their departure. As Rebekah and her servants rode away on their camels, her family ran along beside them. They called out their blessings and wished her many descendants.

Rebekah arrived at Abraham's house just as night was falling. Looking out over the fields, she saw Isaac walking there. She covered her face with her veil and walked shyly toward him. Isaac reached out and took her hand.

Soon after, Isaac married Rebekah, and he loved her with all his heart.

Jacob and Esau

(Genesis 25–30)

As the years passed, Rebekah and Isaac had no children. Isaac prayed that God would grant them a child. God heard Isaac's prayer, and soon Rebekah was pregnant with twins. The first child to be born was a boy named Esau. He had a red complexion and a red, hairy body. Esau's twin brother, Jacob, was born next, holding on to Esau's heel.

As the twins grew up, Jacob became his mother's favorite. He was a quiet boy who liked to stay home. Esau was his father's favorite son, for he was a good hunter and always brought home game for the family to eat.

One day Esau came in from the fields and smelled a delicious stew that Jacob was cooking. "Give me some of your stew. I am famished!" Esau said.

"First you must give me all the special rights that are yours since you are the firstborn son," said Jacob, "and then I will give you some stew."

"My rights will do me no good if I die from hunger!" Esau said. He promised to give his birthright to Jacob.

Then, after he had gobbled up the food, Esau returned to the fields.

As the years passed, Isaac became nearly blind. Before he died, he called Esau to him. "My death could come at any time," Isaac said to his oldest son. "But go into the fields with your bow and arrow and shoot some game for me. After I eat it, I will give you my blessings before I die."

Rebekah overheard their conversation. She hurried to tell Jacob while Esau was hunting. "Now do as I say," she said. "Go into the fields and bring me two baby goats. I will prepare the goat stew that your father loves. Then he will bless you instead of Esau before he dies."

Jacob was puzzled. "My brother is a hairy man and I am not," he said. "What if Father touches me and feels my smooth skin? Then he will curse me rather than bless me."

"I will take on your curse," Rebekah said. "Just do as I say."

When Jacob returned with the goats, she made him put on Esau's clothes. Then she covered his hands and neck with goatskin.

Jacob went into Isaac's room with the goat stew. "My father," he said, "I am your son Esau, your firstborn. I have done as you asked. Please sit up and eat the game I have brought and give me your blessing."

Isaac asked Jacob to come closer. "Your voice sounds like Jacob's," he said, "but your hands feel like Esau's. Are you really Esau?"

"I am, Father," Jacob answered.

Isaac asked Jacob to come closer and kiss him. As Jacob kissed him, Isaac smelled his clothes. They smelled like the earth and fields.

Isaac then blessed Jacob, saying, "My son smells like the fields that God has blessed. May God give you the dew of heaven and the fatness of the earth and plenty of grain and wine. Let nations and people bow down and serve you. Be lord over your brother. Anyone who harms you will be cursed, and everyone who blesses you will be blessed."

When Esau returned from the hunt, he cooked the game he had shot. As his father had asked, he took it to him. "Father, rise and eat the game I brought so that I might have your blessing," he said.

"Who are you?" Isaac asked.

"I am Esau, your oldest son."

Isaac trembled violently. "Then who has already hunted game and come to me and been blessed?"

When Esau heard this, he knew at once that his brother had stolen his blessing, and he cried out in anguish. He rushed to his father and pleaded with him, "Bless me also, my father!"

Isaac realized with horror that he had been tricked into giving his special blessing to Jacob. He knew that by law he could not bless Esau in the same way.

Esau was heartbroken. "First Jacob took my birthright, and now he has taken my blessing," he said. "Have you not saved a blessing for me? Is that the only blessing that can be given?"

Sadly, Isaac could not give his firstborn his blessing. "You will live away from the richness of the earth, Esau," he said. "You will serve your brother and live by your sword. But then you will break free and not be forced to serve him any longer."

Esau's heart filled with hatred. He began to plot Jacob's death. When Rebekah discovered this, she told Jacob to flee to her brother Laban's house in Haran. Rebekah advised Jacob to remain there until Esau's anger had cooled.

Jacob quickly left his family and began the journey to Haran. He walked until it was dark, and then he lay down and, using a stone for a pillow, fell asleep.

As Jacob slept, he dreamed about a great
ladder that reached from heaven to earth. Angels
were climbing up and down the ladder. God
stood at the very top.

"I am the Lord, the God of
Abraham and the God of Isaac,"
God said. "The land upon which
you sleep I will give to you and
your descendants. I will always
be with you. Wherever you go,
I will bring you back to this
land. I will not leave
you until I have kept
this promise."

When Jacob woke up the next morning, he was filled with awe. He named the place where he had slept Bethel, which means "House of God." Then Jacob made a vow: "If God protects me and lets me return to my father's home in peace, I will be faithful to Him and give Him a tenth of all my wealth."

Jacob continued on his journey. When he drew close to Haran, he saw a girl caring for her father's sheep. She was Laban's daughter Rachel. Jacob spent a month at Laban's house, and during that time, he fell deeply in love with Rachel.

One day Jacob went to Rachel's father. "If I work for you for seven years, will you allow Rachel to marry me?"

"Yes," said Laban.

Jacob's love for Rachel was so deep that the years went by as quickly as days. At the end of seven years, Jacob went to Laban to ask for Rachel's hand.

Laban gathered all the men of Haran for a big wedding celebration. But that evening, he played a trick on Jacob. He took Leah, Rachel's older sister, into Jacob's tent, instead of Rachel.

As Leah's face was hidden by a veil, Jacob did not discover that he had married Leah instead of Rachel until the next morning.

Furious, Jacob hurried to Laban. "What have you done to me?" he cried. "You have tricked me! I worked all these years to marry Rachel!"

"In our country, the older girl marries before the younger one," said Laban. "Serve me another seven years, and I will give Rachel to you."

Jacob served Laban for another seven years. Then he married Rachel. Leah gave Jacob six sons and a daughter, but Rachel remained childless. Finally, God answered her prayers and sent her a son. Rachel named the boy Joseph.

Jacob and the Angel
(Genesis 31–33)

Jacob stayed with Laban for twenty years. In those years, he grew rich raising sheep and cattle. One night God came to Jacob in a dream and told him to return to the land of his birth.

Jacob knew Laban would be angry if he left. So when Laban was away, Jacob rounded up his own cattle and sheep. Taking his two wives and twelve children and all his animals and servants, Jacob headed for Gilead.

When Laban discovered that Jacob was gone, he was filled with fury. He and his men followed Jacob for seven days. In that time, God calmed Laban's hatred. So when Laban finally caught up with Jacob, they settled their quarrel and parted as friends.

Jacob sent messengers ahead to his twin brother, Esau. "Tell Esau that I am coming with all my cattle, servants, and family," Jacob told them. "And that I pray he will greet me without anger."

When the messengers returned to Jacob, they told him that Esau was coming to meet him with four hundred men.

Jacob was terrified. He divided his people into two groups, for he thought that if Esau destroyed one group, the other might escape. Then Jacob asked God for help. "Deliver me, please, from the hand of my brother," he prayed.

He took two hundred and twenty goats, two hundred and twenty sheep, thirty camels, forty cows, ten bulls, and thirty donkeys and gave them to his messengers.

"When you meet Esau, give him these animals and say they are gifts from his brother, who is following close behind," Jacob said.

That night Jacob sent his family across the river Jabbok for safekeeping. When Jacob was alone, a stranger appeared. Silently the man approached Jacob and, without a word, began to wrestle with him. As they wrestled silently all night, Jacob realized the stranger was an angel.

At dawn the angel said, "Let me go, for day is breaking."

"I will not let you go unless you bless me," Jacob said.

"What is your name?" the angel asked.

"My name is Jacob," said Jacob.

"From now on, you will be called Israel, which means 'one who strives with God,'" said the angel. Then the angel departed, and Jacob realized that he had seen God face to face.

When the sun rose, Jacob saw Esau heading his way with four hundred men. Jacob crossed the river and quickly divided his children among Leah and Rachel and their maids. He walked ahead of his large family, bowing to the ground seven times as he approached his brother Esau.

Esau ran up to Jacob and embraced him. Together they wept. "Who are these people you have brought with you?" Esau asked.

"This is my family, the children whom God has graciously given your servant," Jacob said. All of Jacob's children and wives bowed down to Esau.

"But why did you send me all of those gifts?" Esau asked.

Jacob explained that he had hoped to please him.

"But I have enough, my brother," Esau said.

Jacob insisted that Esau accept everything he had offered. "When I saw your face just now, it was like seeing the face of God," said Jacob.

Joseph and His Brothers

(Genesis 37–41)

Jacob had twelve sons. His favorite was Joseph, his first son by his wife Rachel. When Joseph was seventeen years old, his father made him a coat of many colors. Jacob's beautiful gift to Joseph made his other sons very jealous of Joseph. They began to hate their brother and spoke unkindly of him.

One night Joseph had a strange dream. The next morning, he told the dream to his brothers. "I dreamed we were binding bushels of wheat in the field and my bushel arose and stood up. Then all of your sheaves gathered around it and bowed down to my sheaf."

Soon after, Joseph reported a second dream to his family: "I dreamed that the sun, the moon, and eleven stars were bowing down to me," he said with wonder.

Joseph's brothers were outraged. Even his father was cross. "Are you to rule us?" they all asked. "Are we to bow down before you?" By now the brothers' jealousy and hatred were deep. Jacob kept his thoughts to himself and wondered what his son's dreams could possibly mean.

One day Jacob sent Joseph to find his brothers, who were tending the herds in the fields near Dothan. When his brothers saw Joseph in the distance, they quickly made a plan to kill him.

"Here comes the dreamer," they said. "Now is the time to kill him and throw his body into a deep pit. We can say that a wild beast has eaten him. That will show him what his dreams were all about!"

Joseph's brother Reuben was troubled. "Let us shed no blood," he begged. "Rather than slay him, we can just throw him into a pit in the wilderness." Reuben had to return home, but he planned to come back later and rescue Joseph from the pit.

As Joseph came upon his brothers, they overpowered him and stripped him of his beautiful robe. Then they grabbed him and threw him into a pit. Afterward they sat down to eat. As they ate, they saw a caravan coming from Gilead on its way to Egypt. The camels in the caravan were loaded down with spices.

Joseph's brother Judah spoke up: "What good is it for us to kill Joseph and hide his body? Come, let's sell him to these traders as a slave. Because he is our brother, we should spare his life." The other brothers agreed.

Joseph's brothers sold him to the traders for twenty pieces of silver, and Joseph was carried away to Egypt. When Reuben later returned and saw Joseph was missing, he tore his clothes in grief and anger.

But Joseph's other brothers were busy planning how they might fool their father. They killed a goat and took Joseph's beautiful robe and dipped it into the goat's blood. Then they took the robe to their father.

"Isn't this Joseph's coat?" they asked the old man.

Jacob recognized it at once. He thought Joseph had been killed by wild beasts. Overwhelmed with grief, Jacob ripped his clothes,

put on sackcloth, and mourned for many days. No one could comfort him.

When the traders arrived in Egypt, they sold Joseph to Potiphar, an officer of Pharaoh, the ruler of Egypt.

Potiphar was pleased with his new servant. He saw that Joseph was a hard worker of unusual intelligence. In time, Potiphar left Joseph completely in charge of his house. God was with him all the time. He blessed all Joseph's work, and Potiphar's house and fields prospered under his hand.

Joseph was not only smart, he was handsome as well. Potiphar's wife fell in love with him and tried to make him fall in love with her, too.

But Joseph resisted her charms. "Your husband trusts me," he said. "He has shared everything with me but his wife. I cannot love you. It would be a great sin against God."

One day Potiphar's wife grabbed Joseph by the sleeve and tried to pull him close to her. Slipping out of his coat, Joseph fled. Seeking revenge, Potiphar's wife ran outside. Even though it was a lie, she shouted, "Help! Joseph forced his way into my room! When I cried out, he ran away!"

Potiphar was so furious that he threw Joseph into prison. While Joseph was held captive, he met the Pharaoh's chief butler and baker, who were also in prison. One night both men had strange dreams.

The butler dreamed about a vine with three branches on it. The branches blossomed into clusters of grapes. "I took the grapes and pressed the juice into Pharaoh's cup," the butler told Joseph.

Joseph knew the meaning of this dream. "The three branches are three days," he said. "Within three days you will be with the Pharaoh again. You will have your old job back. When this comes true, please remember me. Tell the Pharaoh you were in jail with a man who was stolen from his own country. Tell him that I am innocent."

Next the baker told Joseph about his dream. "I dreamed I had three baskets stacked on top of my head," he said. "The top basket held baked goods for the Pharaoh, and birds were eating out of it."

After the man told Joseph his dream, Joseph spoke sadly to him. "The three baskets are three days. Pharaoh will hang you in three days, and the birds will eat your flesh."

Within three days, everything Joseph predicted came true. The unlucky baker was hanged, and the butler returned to Pharaoh's service. But unfortunately, the butler forgot to mention Joseph to the Pharaoh, and Joseph remained in jail.

After Joseph had been in jail for two years, Pharaoh had two troubling dreams. First, Pharaoh dreamed he was standing by the river Nile when seven fat, sleek cows came out of the water and began to eat grass. Then seven thin and gaunt cows came out of the Nile and ate up the fat cows.

Next Pharaoh dreamed that seven spears of plump grain were growing on one stalk. Suddenly seven poor and thin spears of wheat sprang up and swallowed the healthy grain.

When Pharaoh woke up from his dreams, he was very worried, and his spirit was troubled. He sent for all the magicians and wise men of Egypt. "What is the meaning of these dreams?" he asked. But no one could tell him.

The butler was standing nearby and heard what Pharaoh had said. "Why, I remember a young Israelite who was in prison with the baker and me," he said. "When we had strange dreams, he interpreted them for us. Everything he predicted came true! The baker was hanged, and I returned to my old job."

Pharaoh summoned Joseph from the dungeon at once. "I hear that you can interpret dreams," he said.

"It is not I who interprets dreams," Joseph said. "I do this by the power of God."

Joseph listened carefully while Pharaoh told him his two dreams. Then Joseph began to explain their meaning. "God is revealing that you will have seven good years of harvest with plenty throughout the land. But then will come seven years of famine. It will be as if there had never been plenty. God sent you these two dreams to show you that the famine is certain to happen. You need to choose someone who is wise to oversee a plan to store food for the time of the famine."

Pharaoh was deeply grateful. "You will be the head of my house," he told the young man. "You will be second-in-command only to me. Everyone must obey your orders."

Before Joseph could speak, Pharaoh took off his special ring and placed it on Joseph's finger. He ordered his servants to bring Joseph clothes of fine linen. Then he hung a gold chain around his neck. He presented Joseph with a good wife, who was Potiphar's daughter, and sent him out to save Egypt.

Joseph set to work at once. He ordered the Egyptians to store as much grain as possible. When the famine came, it affected people everywhere. But because of Joseph's good and hard work, the people of Egypt had plenty to eat. They even had enough food left over to sell to people who came from far away.

Joseph's Brothers Visit Egypt

(Genesis 42–46)

hen the famine spread to Canaan, Jacob was afraid he and his family would starve to death.

"Why are you doing nothing?" Jacob asked his sons. "Go to Egypt and buy grain for us so that we can survive."

Ten of Jacob's sons left for Egypt. But Jacob was afraid to let his youngest son, Benjamin, go with them, so he kept him at home.

When the brothers arrived in Egypt, they went before Joseph, who was in charge of giving out the grain. Joseph's brothers did not recognize him. Believing he was an important Egyptian, they bowed down in front of him with their faces to the ground. Joseph knew at once who they were, but he hid his feelings and pretended they were strangers.

"Where are you from?" Joseph asked in a harsh voice. When the brothers told him they were from Canaan, Joseph appeared to be angry and suspicious. "You are spies," he said coldly. "You have come to spy on us."

The brothers shrank back in fear. "No, we are honest men! We have never been spies! We are all the sons of one man. Our youngest

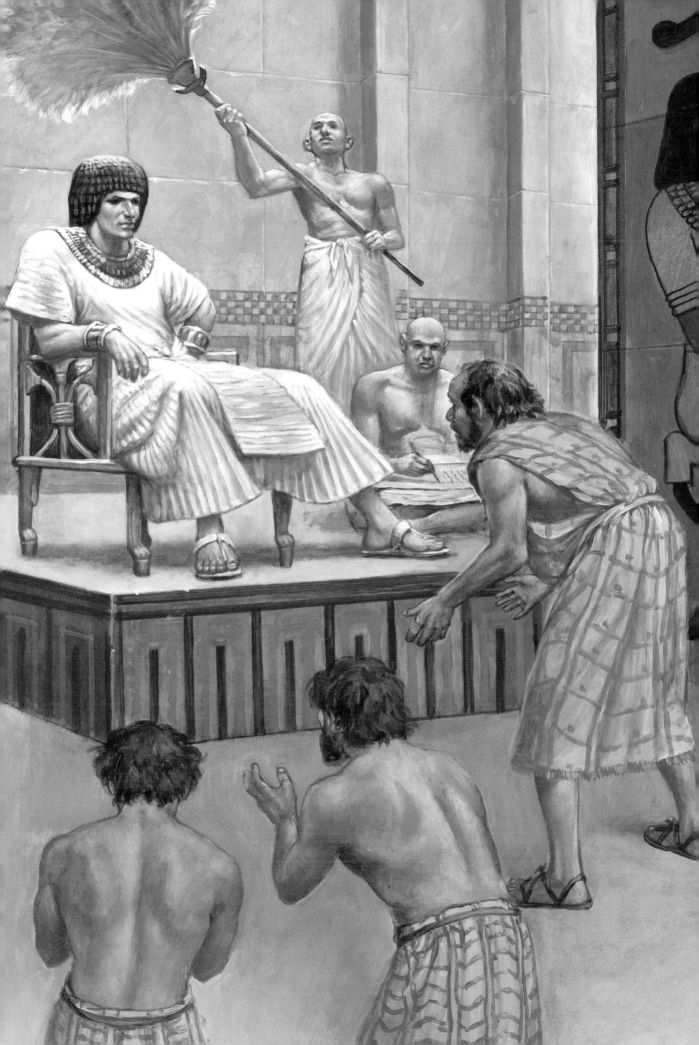

brother is at home with our father, and our other brother is dead. We have only come to buy grain."

Joseph decided to put his brothers to a test. "If you ever want to leave here, one of you must go and get your youngest brother," he said. "But first you are all going to prison for three days until I send for you again."

Three days later, Joseph sent for his brothers. He gave them wheat. Again he demanded that they bring their youngest brother back to Egypt. "If you do not, I will put you to death!" Joseph said. "I'm keeping one of you as hostage to make sure you obey me."

"It is because of our great wrong against Joseph that we are being punished," they whispered to each other in their own language.

They didn't realize that Joseph could understand everything they said. Their distress touched him greatly, and he turned away to hide his tears.

As his brothers talked among themselves, Joseph seized the one named Simeon and had him tied up. He ordered his servants to fill his brothers' bags with grain. Joseph also ordered that the money they used to pay for the grain be hidden in their sacks.

The brothers loaded their donkeys with the sacks of grain and left for Canaan. As they stopped to feed the animals, one brother discovered the money in his sack. "What is this?" he cried fearfully. "What has God done to us?"

Joseph's brothers returned home. In tears, they told their father what had happened.

"I have lost Joseph and Simeon," said Jacob, "and now you want to take away another son. I will never allow you to take Benjamin, for I will die of grief if anything should ever happen to him."

The famine in Canaan was severe, and the grain quickly ran out.

Once more Jacob gathered his sons and told them to return to Egypt for more food.

"But we were warned we had to bring Benjamin back with us," said Judah.

When Jacob protested, Judah tried to reassure his father. "Please let us take Benjamin," he said. "I will be responsible for bringing him home safely. If anything happens to him, the blame will be on my head forever."

Reluctantly Jacob agreed. He told his sons to take gifts of fruits, nuts, and honey. He also told them to take twice the payment they had taken before and asked them to give back the money they had discovered in their sacks.

The brothers returned to Egypt with their youngest brother, Benjamin. When Joseph heard of their arrival, he ordered his servants to prepare a feast, and he invited his brothers to his house. Fearfully they told Joseph's steward about the money they had found in their sacks.

The steward's answer surprised them. "Your God must have put treasure in your sacks for you," he said. "You gave me money when you were here before." Then the steward brought their brother Simeon out to them.

Joseph soon arrived, and his brothers presented their gifts to him. When Joseph saw Benjamin, he was overcome with emotion and left the room to weep. After he washed his face, he invited his guests to dinner. He gave Benjamin five times the food he gave the others.

After dinner Joseph ordered his servants to put the money back into the brothers' sacks. He also ordered them to put a silver cup into Benjamin's.

As they rode away, Joseph sent his steward to stop the brothers and search their belongings. The steward found the money and the silver cup. The brothers were so scared they tore their clothes in despair. When they were brought back to face Joseph, they fell to the ground.

"What have you done?" Joseph demanded angrily. He ordered his brothers to return home, but he demanded that they leave Benjamin behind in Egypt.

Judah stepped forward. "We promised our father we would return with our brother Benjamin. Our father is an old man, and his happiness depends on the well-being of the boy. Please let me stay in his place. If we return without our brother, I cannot bear the pain that would come upon our father."

Joseph ordered everyone, except his brothers, out of the room. "I am Joseph, your brother," he said, weeping. The brothers could hardly believe what he was saying, and they were speechless.

Joseph hugged Benjamin and kissed each of his brothers. He asked them to go back to Canaan and return with their families.

When Jacob's sons returned home with the good news about Joseph, the old man was overjoyed. "My son is still alive!" cried Jacob. "I must see him before I die!"

Jacob's family gathered all their possessions and returned at once to make their home in Egypt. At long last, Jacob was joyfully reunited with his beloved lost son.

The Birth of Moses

(Exodus 1–2)

Because Jacob's name had been changed by God to Israel, the descendants of Abraham, Isaac, and Jacob came to be called Israelites. Many years passed. Long after Joseph died, a new Pharaoh was ruling Egypt, and the Egyptians began treating the Israelites badly. The Egyptians had become fearful that the Israelites might side with Egypt's enemies in case of war.

To keep the Israelites under control, the Egyptians made them work like slaves. They suffered greatly. But the worst was yet to come. The Pharaoh ordered that all baby boys born into an Israelite family were to be drowned in the river Nile.

An Israelite woman desperately tried to save her three-month-old son from this terrible fate. She put the baby in a waterproof basket and placed the basket in the reeds at the edge of the river. She then told his sister Miriam to stay close by and watch out for her baby brother.

Soon after, the Pharaoh's daughter came to bathe in the river with her servants. She found the basket hidden in the bulrushes.

When the young woman pulled back the blankets, she was amazed. Snuggled inside the basket was a beautiful baby boy. The baby began crying. Pharaoh's daughter was deeply moved and took pity on him.

Miriam stepped forward from her hiding place. "Shall I go and get a nurse to help you take care of the child?" she asked. Pharaoh's daughter eagerly accepted her offer.

Miriam then raced home to get her mother. When the mother arrived, Pharaoh's daughter asked her to take the baby home and care for him.

For several years, the boy stayed in his mother's house. Then he was sent to live with Pharaoh's daughter, who loved him like a son. She named the boy Moses, which means "to draw up," for she had drawn him up out of the water.

Moses and the Burning Bush

(Exodus 2–4)

hen Moses was a young man, he saw an Egyptian beating an Israelite. Furious to see one of his people cruelly mistreated, Moses killed the Egyptian. Thinking no one was watching him, he hid the man's body in the sand.

The next day, Moses saw two Israelites fighting and tried to stop them. One of the men turned on him and said, "Who made you ruler and judge over us? Are you going to kill us like you killed that Egyptian?" Moses knew his crime had been discovered.

When word of it got back to Pharaoh, he ordered that Moses be killed. So Moses fled to the land of Midian. He was sitting by a well when seven young women came to water their father's flock. A group of shepherds rushed up and drove the women away. But Moses stepped forward and bravely drew water to fill the women's jugs.

The women were the daughters of Jethro, a priest in Midian. When Jethro heard about Moses's brave deed, he told his daughters to invite him to their home. Jethro soon grew so fond of Moses that he asked him to live with his family. He even gave Moses his daughter Zipporah to wed.

Moses was in the wilderness, tending Jethro's flock, when a bush nearby burst into flames. Even though the bush was on fire, it wasn't burned up in the flames.

Suddenly Moses heard the voice of God coming from the burning bush. "Moses, Moses," God called.

"Here I am," Moses answered.

"Moses, do not come any closer!" God said. "I am the God of Isaac and the God of Jacob. Take off your shoes. You are standing on holy ground!"

Moses did as God said. He was so terrified he covered his face, because he was afraid to look at God.

"I have seen the suffering of my people in Egypt, and I have heard their cries," said God. "I have come to free them from the Egyptians. The Israelites will go to a good land, a land flowing with milk and honey. You will lead them out of Egypt."

Moses was terrified. He could not imagine that one as ordinary as he could carry out such a great task.

"Do not be afraid, for I will be with you," God promised.

"But when the people ask me who sent me, what should I say?" said Moses.

"I AM WHO I AM," God answered mysteriously. "When you go to the people of Israel, tell them I AM sent you—the one who is always there. Tell the Elders of the Israelites that the God of your fathers, the God of Abraham and Isaac and Jacob, sent you. After that, you must go to Pharaoh. Tell him to let your people go. I know he will not listen, and I will make horrible things happen in Egypt. Then he will grant your request."

God gave Moses powers to help convince the Israelites to follow him. "Take your staff in your hand," God commanded, "and throw it down. It will become a serpent."

Moses did as God said, and his staff became a serpent.

"Now take the snake by the tail," the voice of God said.

When Moses picked up the serpent, it turned back into a wooden staff.

God then told Moses to put his hand inside his tunic. When Moses pulled it out, his hand was white as snow. He put his hand back into his tunic, and his hand returned to normal. God said that if the people still didn't want to follow him, he should pour some water from the river Nile on the ground and it would turn into blood.

Even with these miracles, Moses was afraid. "I cannot speak clearly," he said to God. "I stutter, and people don't understand me."

"Your brother Aaron speaks well," said God. "Let Aaron say the words that are in your heart." Then God commanded Moses to take up his staff and be on his way.

Let My People Go!

(Exodus 5–12)

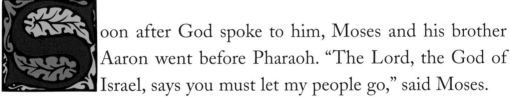

oon after God spoke to him, Moses and his brother Aaron went before Pharaoh. "The Lord, the God of Israel, says you must let my people go," said Moses.

Pharaoh scoffed at Moses's request. "Who is this God who orders me to let the Israelites go?" he asked.

Pharaoh then told his overseers to stop giving the Israelite slaves the straw they needed to make bricks for Egypt. Instead the Israelites would have to find their own straw and still make as many bricks as they had before.

The Israelites scattered throughout the countryside trying to gather bits of straw. When they couldn't make bricks quickly enough, the Egyptians beat them without mercy.

In despair, the Israelites went to Moses and Aaron. "Why have you brought this trouble upon us?" they asked. "Because of you, the Egyptians hate us now and will surely kill us!"

Moses sought an answer from God. "Why have you mistreated these people?" he asked. "Why did you send me here?"

"I have heard the groaning of the people of Israel and I have remembered my covenant," said God. "I am the Lord. I will bring you out of Egypt and give you the land I promised to Abraham, Isaac, and Jacob. Go back to Pharaoh. Ask him again to let the people of Israel go."

Moses and Aaron returned to Pharaoh, but again he refused their request. Then he ordered the two men to perform a miracle. Moses signaled Aaron to throw his staff to the ground, and immediately the staff turned into a serpent!

Pharaoh quickly ordered his own sorcerers and wise men to throw their staffs to the ground. By using trickery, they also turned their staffs into serpents. But Moses's serpent quickly swallowed up the serpents of the sorcerers. Still Pharaoh would not listen to Moses and Aaron. He would not let the Israelites go.

Every morning Pharaoh walked along the river Nile. One day God commanded Moses to take his staff and meet Pharaoh by the water. When Moses saw Pharaoh, he said, "The Lord, God of the Israelites, has sent me to you to tell you that you must let my people go. But you have not listened and have disobeyed him."

As God commanded, Moses hit the water with his staff, and the river turned red with blood. Fish died and floated to the surface. Soon all the water in Egypt turned into blood, and nobody could drink it. People were forced to scratch in the ground in search of water.

After seven days, Moses and Aaron returned to Pharaoh, and again they asked him to let the Israelites go. They told him a plague of frogs would come from the Nile and cover the land. But Pharaoh was not moved.

Soon all of Egypt was covered with millions of frogs! The frogs crawled and jumped everywhere. They hopped into people's houses, beds, ovens, and even bread bowls.

Desperate, Pharaoh promised to let the Israelites go if Moses

would rid Egypt of the frogs. Moses asked God to end the plague, and heaps of dead and dying frogs piled up everywhere. When Pharaoh saw there was relief from the frogs, he refused again to let the Israelites go.

Next, at God's command, Aaron hit the dust with his staff. The dust turned into gnats! The gnats spread over the land, biting all the people and animals. Everyone was in torment. "This is the finger of God," the priests warned Pharaoh.

Pharaoh begged Moses to end this terrible plague. But after the gnats had disappeared, Pharaoh once again broke his promise and would not let the Israelites go.

Then God sent a plague of flies to Egypt. The flies swarmed into houses and covered the people. They stung their faces and buzzed in their hair. Pharaoh once again begged for Moses's help. When the plague ended, Pharaoh refused to free the Israelites.

God sent a new plague. This time all the cattle that belonged to the Egyptians began to die, while all the cattle of the Israelites remained healthy. Still Pharaoh would not let Moses's people go.

God then commanded Moses to take handfuls of ashes and throw them into the air. The ashes became dust that drifted over all of the land. As the dust fell to earth, people and animals broke out in painful boils and sores.

Pharaoh still would not change his mind. God told Moses to stretch out his hand toward heaven. Dreadful thunder shook the sky, and hailstones rained down on Egypt. All the plants were destroyed. Every tree was stripped bare by the force of the hail. Shredded leaves lay piled up along the streets and roads.

At long last, Pharaoh's heart seemed to open. "Enough of this thunder!" he said to Moses. "I have sinned this time. The Lord is in the right. You and your people do not have to stay here any longer."

"Then I will leave the city," said Moses, "and when I stretch out my hands to the Lord, the thunder will cease at once." Moses walked away from the city and stretched out his hands, and the thunder and hail immediately stopped.

In order to teach Pharaoh a lesson, God hardened his heart yet again, and once more Pharaoh refused to let the Israelites leave. Moses then took his rod and lifted it to the sky. An east wind began to blow, and it blew hard all through the night.

The next morning, the Egyptians woke up and saw a black cloud covering the sky. Millions of locusts were blotting out the sun! The insects crawled over the fields, devouring all the plants. They ate up all the fruit that had been spared by the hail. Finally, not a green living thing was left in the land of Egypt.

Pharaoh begged Moses and Aaron to stop the plague of locusts. Moses asked God for help, and soon a strong west wind drove all the locusts into the Red Sea.

Once again Pharaoh refused to allow the Israelites to leave Egypt. God then commanded Moses to stretch out his hand toward heaven. When Moses did this, a thick darkness fell over Egypt for three days.

Again Pharaoh called for Moses. "Go! Take your people, even your children, but leave your flocks and your herds behind!" he said.

Moses refused Pharaoh's offer. Pharaoh was furious and ordered Moses to get out of his sight. "If I ever see you again, you will die!" he shouted.

Again God spoke to Moses. "I will bring one more plague upon Pharaoh and Egypt," God said. "After that, he will let you go."

God told Moses to prepare his people to leave Egypt. He said that at midnight, the Angel of Death would descend to visit all the houses of Egypt, and the oldest child of every family would die.

But God wanted to protect his people. He gave Moses instructions to make sure all the Israelite children would be safe. That night all the Israelite families killed a lamb. They ate it with bitter herbs and unleavened bread, and sprinkled their doorframes with the lamb's blood. God promised that the Angel of Death would then pass over any houses marked with the blood of the lamb, and leave the oldest child unharmed.

Moses ordered the Israelites to stay in their houses that night. At midnight, when the streets were still, the Angel of Death went through all of Egypt. The angel spared no Egyptian home. The firstborn of all the Egyptians began to sicken and die. Even the Pharaoh's eldest son died.

Pharaoh rose from his bed to hear great cries of anguish. The people of Egypt were overwhelmed with grief and sorrow.

Pharaoh sent for Moses at once. Finally, he could bear the plagues sent by God no more. He ordered Moses to take his people and leave.

The Israelites rushed about frantically, gathering their children and flocks of animals. Women hurried around their houses, packing up the family's possessions. They even took unbaked loaves of bread out of their ovens.

Then Moses led six hundred thousand Israelites out of the land of Egypt.

"Remember this day and this moment," Moses said to his people. "This is the day you came out of Egypt and out of the house of bondage. By the strength of his hand, God brought you out of this land." God ordered that each year the Israelites' descendants should hold a feast to celebrate the end of their captivity in Egypt.

The Parting of the Red Sea

(Exodus 13–15)

oses and his people left Egypt, carrying the bones of their ancestor Joseph. They traveled by day and night. During the day, God went before them in a pillar of cloud to show the way. At night the cloud became a pillar of fire to lead the Israelites through the darkness.

After the Israelites had departed, Pharaoh's heart hardened once more. He ordered his soldiers to leap into their chariots and chase after the fleeing hordes of people.

When the Israelites got to the Red Sea, they saw the dust of the Egyptian chariots pursuing them. Terrified, they rushed to Moses. "What have you done? Have you taken us out of Egypt only to watch us die in the wilderness?" they cried.

"Do not be afraid, stand firm!" said Moses. "The Lord will protect you. You will never see the Egyptians again. The Lord will fight for you."

God told Moses to lift up his rod and stretch his hand out over the sea. As he spoke, the pillar of cloud moved behind

60

the Israelites. The cloud was so dark that the Egyptians could no longer see.

As night fell, Moses stretched out his hand over the sea. A strong wind began to blow from the east. It blew all night, driving back the waters until the Red Sea parted, making a dry path for the Israelites. All night the Israelites crossed the sea between the great walls of water that rose up on either side of them.

When dawn broke, the Egyptian army flew into a panic when they realized what had happened. They leapt into their chariots and tried to follow the Israelites. Moses stretched out his hand once more, and the sea closed around Pharaoh's soldiers, covering all of the chariots and all of the horses and drowning the entire army.

The Israelites were filled with wonder and awe, for they knew that the power of God had saved them. Moses's sister Miriam pulled out a tambourine. "Sing to the Lord, for he has triumphed gloriously; horse and rider he has thrown into the sea!" she shouted. The Israelites all began dancing and singing for joy, all the while giving great thanks to God and praising his name.

The Ten Commandments

(Exodus 16–20)

or several weeks, the Israelites wandered in the searing heat of the Sinai wilderness. As they grew hungry and exhausted, they began to despair. They gathered in groups to whisper and complain about Moses and Aaron.

"Were we led into this wilderness only to die of starvation?" they asked. "We should have died in Egypt. At least we had enough bread to eat there."

Knowing the Israelites were desperate, God promised Moses that he would soon provide food for everyone.

Moses called his people together. "Fear not," he said. "God has promised to provide for all of you. Every evening you will have meat, and in the morning you will have as much bread as you can eat."

The next morning, there was heavy dew. When the dew evaporated, strange round flakes covered the ground. "What is this?" the Israelites asked one another.

"This is called manna," said Moses. "It is the bread that God has promised you. Each day God will send you a fresh supply. But you must gather only as much manna as you need for each day."

The Israelites began to pick up the manna and hesitantly eat it. The manna tasted like wafers flavored with coriander and honey. It was delicious!

Some people were anxious, though, and did not trust God. They tried to save enough manna to last for more days. But to their dismay, their manna had become black and wormy.

The Israelites now had food, because God kept his promise to send manna every day. But as they wandered, they found it hard to find fresh water, and grew very thirsty. Soon they confronted Moses again. "Why have you brought us out of Egypt, only for our children and cattle to die of thirst?" they asked.

The Israelites' anger frightened Moses. Again he turned to God. "My people are ready to stone me!" he said.

God told Moses to take the leaders of the Israelites up to Mount Horeb. There, God said, they would find a rock. He told Moses to hit the rock with his rod. When Moses did this, fresh cool water poured out of the rock, and the thirsty Israelites rushed forward to drink their fill.

For another three months, the Israelites wandered in the wilderness. Finally, they stopped near Mount Sinai. Moses climbed the mountain to be alone with God.

"I have brought you out of Egypt on the wings of eagles," said God. "If you obey me now and keep your promise with me, you will be my treasure above all others. Tell the people I will speak to them in three days. They should wash their clothes and prepare to hear me."

On the third day, everyone was ready and waiting to hear God. Suddenly there were a roar of thunder and flashes of lightning. Thick clouds covered the mountaintop, and a blast of trumpets rang out. The people were so frightened they began to tremble.

God descended upon the mountain in a cloud of fire and smoke.

The mountain glowed red hot like a furnace and began to quake. As the people cowered in fear, God called Moses up to him.

Then Moses disappeared into the clouds, and God spoke to him, saying:

"I am the Lord your God, who brought you out of the land of Egypt, out of the house of bondage.

"You shall have no other gods before me.

"You shall not worship any statue or idol, or anything found on the earth.

"You shall speak my name with respect and awe, and not in vain.

"You shall remember the Sabbath, or seventh day, and keep it holy.

"You shall honor your father and mother.

"You shall not kill.

"You shall be faithful to your wife or husband.

"You shall not steal.

"You shall not lie and bear false witness against your neighbor.

"You shall not be jealous and covet other people's things."

As thunder roared and lightning flashed, the Israelites below Mount Sinai were filled with fear and wonder. But Moses soon appeared to calm them. "Do not be afraid," he said. "God has come to test you and show you his power, so you will obey his commandments and stay free from sin."

Moses then returned to the presence of God. Again his people lost sight of him as he disappeared behind the thick clouds covering the mountaintop.

The Golden Calf

(Exodus 32, 35–40)

Moses stayed hidden on top of Mount Sinai for forty days and forty nights. The people grew worried and went to Aaron, saying, "You must make gods for us to worship. We do not know what has become of Moses."

Aaron considered their request. "Give me all your golden jewelry," he finally said. Aaron built a huge fire, melted the jewelry, and fashioned it into a golden calf. The people built an altar to worship it.

The next day, the Israelites rose early and prayed to the calf. They sacrificed burnt offerings and feasted, drank, and danced wildly in front of the altar.

When God saw this, he grew angry. "Go down to your people!" he ordered Moses. "Your people have already turned away from my commandments! I will destroy them!"

Moses asked God to forgive the Israelites and raced down the mountain into the camp. When he arrived, he was horrified to see everyone dancing madly and singing in front of the golden calf.

Moses was carrying two tablets with God's Ten Commandments engraved on them. In a rage, he dashed the tablets to the ground, and they shattered into pieces. A hush fell over the crowd as Moses then hurled the golden calf into the fire.

Then Moses ground the ashes to powder, scattered them on water, and made the Israelites drink it.

"Whoever is on God's side and my side, come and stand by me!" he shouted.

There was silence. Only the tribe of Levi stepped forward. Moses ordered the Levites to kill other men in camp. That night the slaughter began. When it was over, three thousand lay dead.

Moses asked God once more to forgive the Israelites.

"Go and lead them," God commanded. "But I will continue to punish your people for worshipping the golden calf."

Soon God spoke to Moses once more. "Cut two stone tablets as you did before. And I will write the Ten Commandments on them again."

Moses did as God said. He rose at dawn and climbed to the top of Mount Sinai, taking the tablets with him. God descended in a cloud, and for the next forty days and nights, Moses stayed in his presence. During this time, God gave him the laws his people were to follow.

When Moses came down from Mount Sinai, he was filled with the glory of God. His face glowed with a strange bright light. When the people saw him, they were frightened. After Moses finished speaking to everyone, he covered his face with a veil. Then he read all of the Ten Commandments to them.

After God gave the Israelites the Ten Commandments, he wanted them to feel his presence. So he told them to build a beautiful tabernacle as a place of worship. The precious stone tablets with the Ten Commandments would stay in the tabernacle in a golden box called the Ark of the Covenant.

God wanted the tabernacle to be filled with beautiful things, so Moses asked everyone to donate any treasures they had. Many offered all their beautiful jewelry, colorful hangings, animal skins, and cloth. Others brought precious objects of silver and gold.

For many months, the Israelites worked on the tabernacle. The tabernacle had to be built so that they could take it down and put it back together whenever they moved.

Workers built two rooms with wooden walls and covered the roof with cloth and animal skins. They built pillars to surround the tabernacle and hung fine linen between the pillars to flutter in the breeze. They made a courtyard with a large altar in the middle.

When it was finished, only the priests and Levites could enter the tabernacle. Smoke drifted up from the altar as they burned animal sacrifices.

Before the priests could enter the tabernacle, they had to wash their hands in a large basin. When their hands were clean, they drew back the long curtains that covered the door. Then the priests stepped into a dimly lit room shimmering with gold.

This was the "Holy Room." It was anointed with special oil, and incense burned on its altar night and day, filling the air with perfume. Candles flickered in the golden and silver candlesticks. Next to the altar, a golden table held loaves of bread that stood for the tribes of Israel.

The second room was the most sacred of all. It housed the Ark of the Covenant, which held the two stone tablets with God's Ten Commandments. This room was called the "Most Holy Place." Only the high priest was allowed inside, and he could enter the room only one day a year, on the Day of Atonement.

Throughout the day, a cloud that held the spirit of God hovered over the tabernacle. At night, the tabernacle filled with a glowing fire so that all of the Israelites could see the glory of God before them wherever they traveled.

A Land of Milk and Honey
(Numbers 13–14)

 hen the Israelites camped in the wilderness of Paran near the land of Canaan, God spoke to Moses: "Send a man from every tribe into the land of Canaan, for this is the land I give to the children of Israel."

Moses gathered together twelve men from the twelve tribes. "Go into southern Canaan and into the mountains," he said. "See what kind of people live there. Are they strong or weak? What is their land like? Do the towns have walls or are they open? Find out about the soil and the trees. And if you can, bring back some fruit."

The spies set off. They spent forty days exploring the new land. They found juicy grapes, pomegranates, and figs in abundance. They loaded up the fruit and carried it back to camp with them. When they returned to their families, everyone clustered about.

"This is a land that flows with milk and honey," the spies said. "So much food grows there! The cities are large and have walls surrounding them. The people seem strong and healthy."

A spy named Caleb stepped forward. "With God's help, we

believe we can take over and occupy the land of Canaan for ourselves," he said.

The other spies, though, drew back in fear. They began to make up lies about what they had seen. "We are like grasshoppers compared to the people of Canaan," they said. "We are facing a land of giants that devours its inhabitants."

The Israelites wept with fear when they heard about the giants of Canaan. They no longer believed what Caleb had said. They grew so angry they even threatened to stone him to death. Many clamored to choose a new leader and return to Egypt.

God saw the people's lack of faith. He told Moses that anyone who had not trusted him would never be allowed to enter the Promised Land. They would be disinherited and plagued by pestilence, and they would die in the wilderness.

Some people changed their minds and decided to march into Canaan. But God was not on their side now. Those who fought were killed or driven back. And for the next forty years, all the Israelites wandered in the wilderness.

Joshua and the Battle of Jericho
(Numbers 27, Deuteronomy 34, Joshua 1–6)

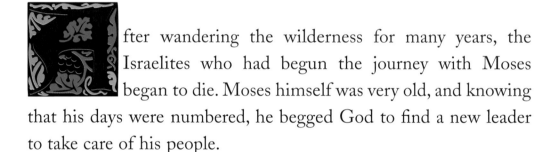fter wandering the wilderness for many years, the Israelites who had begun the journey with Moses began to die. Moses himself was very old, and knowing that his days were numbered, he begged God to find a new leader to take care of his people.

God chose a good and spirit-filled man named Joshua. Moses gathered his people together one last time. Then he called Joshua and Eleazar, the priest, to stand before him. Moses laid his hands on Joshua's head. This was the sign that God wanted Joshua to lead the people of Israel.

Moses wrote down all the things he wanted his people to know about worship, feasts, and offerings. Then he blessed them. Full of grief, the Israelites watched their old leader walk away. Moses slowly made his way up to the top of Mount Pisgah. From there, he gazed out in all directions over the deserts, the valleys, and the cities. He saw a beautiful land that stretched all the way to the Mediterranean Sea.

God then spoke to Moses. "All the land as far as you can see will belong to your descendants. But you yourself will not cross over into the land that will be the home of your people."

Moses died on the mountaintop. Joshua knew the Israelites would never see a leader like Moses again. Moses was the one man who had met God face to face, and had done wonderful things for his people. For thirty days, the Israelites were in deep mourning.

Then one day the Lord spoke to Joshua. Soon after, Joshua called the Israelites together. "Pack up all your things," he said. "In three days we will cross over the Jordan River and enter the Promised Land."

Joshua ordered the men to arm for war and the women to stay in camp. While the people were gathering their animals and possessions together, Joshua sent two spies to slip into the city of Jericho.

When the spies were inside the walls of Jericho, they needed a place to stay. They were pleased when a woman named Rahab invited them to spend the night in her house.

The people of Jericho were frightened. They knew the Israelites had camped across the Jordan and wanted their lands. The king of Jericho learned about the spies and quickly ordered that the gates of the city be closed and locked. Then he sent messengers to Rahab, demanding she send the spies out of her house.

Rahab hid the men under stalks of grain that were drying on her roof. She told the messengers the men had left.

"I know the Lord has given you this land and that the Israelites can conquer Jericho," she told the men as soon as the messengers had gone. "The people here are afraid and weak. When you capture the city, please bring no harm to me or my family. Give me a sign of good faith."

The spies were grateful to Rahab, so they told her to hang a crimson cord from her window. This would be a sign for the Israelites to spare her household.

Rahab's house stood just inside the walls of the city. She rushed to find a strong rope, and she used the rope to lower the men over the wall.

When the spies returned safely to Joshua, they gave him information about Jericho. Joshua felt confident the Israelites could capture the city, so he prepared his people to cross the Jordan River.

Joshua ordered twelve priests to carry the Ark of the Covenant ahead of the Israelites. "Everyone must stay far behind the Ark!" he said. "As soon as the feet of the priests touch the water, the river will stop flowing and a path will appear, which you should all follow."

Slowly the procession began to move forward. When the priests arrived at the river, they began to wade into the water. As God had promised, at once the river stopped flowing, and a clear path led the people between great walls of water.

All the Israelites passed safely into the Promised Land. When they reached the plains of Jericho, forty thousand Israelites prepared for battle. As they marched toward Jericho, they could see the gates of the city bolted shut.

"March around the city walls once a day for six days. Carry the Ark of the Covenant behind you," God told Joshua. "The seven priests who walk before the Ark should hold trumpets made of rams' horns."

For six days, the Israelites walked around the city walls once a day. On the seventh day, the men circled six times. As they walked, the fearful people inside the city only heard the steady *tramp, tramp* of footsteps. Then, as the men walked around for the seventh time, trumpet blasts shattered the air.

All the Israelites began shouting. Their cries mixed with the mighty blasts of the trumpets. With a great roar, the walls of Jericho began to shake and tremble. Then all at once the walls came tumbling down.

Through the blur of the dust, the Israelites saw the open city. They rushed over the rubble and set fire to all the buildings, saving only those things made of gold, silver, bronze, and iron.

That day all the people of Jericho died except for Rahab and her family. After she and her family were rescued, they peacefully lived out their lives among the Israelites in the Promised Land of milk and honey.

Deborah Leads Her People

(Judges 2–5)

or years, the Israelites prospered under the leadership of Joshua. But after he died, many people turned away from God and began to worship idols instead. When Jabin, the king of Canaan, saw that the Israelites had become weak, he attacked them. Because they had forsaken God, the Israelites lost many battles and suffered under King Jabin's harsh rule.

During this time, a woman and revered prophetess named Deborah remained loyal to God. Deborah was so wise that she was made a judge of Israel. During the day, she would often sit under the shade of a palm tree and give counsel to those who came to see her.

Aware that the Israelites lived in great misery, God chose to give them another chance. After God told Deborah his plan, she sent for a brave man named Barak.

"Call together ten thousand men," Deborah told Barak. "Go with them to Mount Tabor. God will get Sisera, who commands Jabin's army, to mount an attack against you. Sisera and his soldiers and chariots will meet you at the Kishon River."

Barak begged for Deborah to come with him. "Of course I will come with you," Deborah promised. "But there is one thing you must know: God will give the final victory over Sisera to a woman and not you."

Sisera soon heard that the Israelite army was waiting to go into battle. He called for nine hundred iron chariots and ordered his men to prepare for war on Mount Tabor.

When Deborah found out that Sisera and his army were on the move, she woke up Barak. "Rise quickly!" she said. "Today, with God's help, you will defeat his army!"

Barak and his men raced down the mountain and attacked the enemy. Sisera's men tried to escape, but they were overtaken and slain. Sisera fled for his life. Desperate, he made his way to a tent owned by a woman named Jael, who invited him inside. "Lie down and sleep," she urged the exhausted general.

Sisera sank down and fell into a deep slumber, and Jael covered him up with a blanket. But Jael felt no pity for the wicked general. She knew all the suffering that he had caused. As Sisera slept, Jael stabbed him in the temple with a tent peg.

Shortly afterward, Barak rushed by, searching for Sisera. "Come in," Jael said. "He is here, but I have slain him."

Deborah and Barak were overjoyed. They knew Jabin's rule over the Israelites was near an end. They burst into song.

"Let all your enemies die like this, O God," they sang. *"But let all your friends be like the sun as it rises in its might!"*

For the next forty years, there was peace in all the land.

God Calls Gideon

(Judges 6–7)

orty years later, the Israelites turned away from God once again and began worshipping idols. God forsook them, and the people of the country of Midian descended upon them.

The Midianites moved onto the Israelites' land with their tents, camels, and flocks. For seven years, they burned the Israelites' wheat, pillaged their houses, and slaughtered their animals. Eventually the Israelites were left with nothing. They had no crops, sheep, cattle, or donkeys. Since they did not even have houses, many had to seek shelter in caves. Now finally in great despair, they remembered God, and cried out to him for help.

God answered their prayers. He sent an angel to an Israelite named Gideon. One day, while Gideon was secretly threshing wheat, the angel appeared and sat near him, beneath an oak tree.

"Gideon, you mighty warrior, God is with you," said the angel. "You will soon save your people from the Midianites."

Gideon did not understand. He was a humble man who came from a poor family. "But how can I do this?" he asked. "My clan is

the weakest in Manasseh, and I am the least in my father's house."

Though the angel assured Gideon that God would help him, Gideon asked for a sign. He then prepared an offering of a young goat and unleavened bread, placed them on a rock, and poured out broth into a pot.

The angel touched Gideon's offerings with a stick—and fire sprang from the rock and burned the offerings! Then the angel of the Lord disappeared.

"I have seen an angel of the Lord face to face!" Gideon cried.

The voice of God answered, saying, "Peace be to you; do not fear, you shall not die."

That same night, Gideon walked to the altar of the Midianites' god, who was named Baal. With the help of oxen and ten men, Gideon ripped the altar apart. In its place, he built an altar and sacrificed an ox to the God of the Israelites.

The next morning, the Midianites were enraged to find their altar in ruins, their sacred pole cut down, and a new altar standing in its place. Word soon spread that Gideon was to blame. Men stormed his father's house to demand that Gideon die.

"Do not worry. Baal will take his own revenge if he is truly a god," Gideon's father told them. The mob calmed down and slowly dispersed.

But for Gideon, this victory was just the beginning. Thirty-two thousand Israelites hurried to join him at the spring of Harod. Gideon called out to his men, "If any of you are afraid, go home now!" Twenty-two thousand returned home, and ten thousand remained.

God then told Gideon to tell the remaining ones to go down to the spring for a drink of water. "Watch how they drink," said God. "Those who lap up the water with their tongues like a dog should stay with you. Those who kneel down to drink the water should be sent home."

After this test, Gideon was left with only three hundred men. That night, he gave each man a trumpet made from a ram's horn. The men also carried burning torches hidden inside pottery jars. They crept up to the enemy's camp and quietly surrounded it. When Gideon gave a signal, all the men blew loudly on their trumpets. Then they broke the pots that held the torches.

Fire and noise filled the dark!

The sleeping Midianites leapt up in terror. In their confusion, they began fighting and killing one another. That night Gideon and his men won a great battle without striking a single blow.

Samson

(Judges 13–14, 16)

or over twenty years, the Israelites continued to love and honor God. Then many of them fell away from God once again. They began to bow down before idols and worship them.

A man named Manoah and his wife remained faithful to God. They were childless until one day an angel appeared to them and promised that they would soon have a son. The angel told them that their son would belong to God, and that his job was to save the Israelites from the Philistines. The angel also warned them never to cut their son's hair.

When the boy was born, he was named Samson. Samson grew up and became known for his incredible strength and bravery. In time, he fell in love with a Philistine woman named Delilah. Since the Philistines were afraid of Samson, they allowed him to travel freely through their land to visit her.

Desperate to know the secret of Samson's great strength, the Philistine rulers sent for Delilah. They promised her many pieces of silver if she would find out Samson's secret so they could capture him.

Delilah decided to use the power of her beauty to make Samson reveal the truth. "What is it that makes you so strong? Tell me how someone might capture you," she said one day to Samson.

Samson told Delilah that if he was tied up with seven new bowstrings that were not dried, he would lose all his powers. "I would then become as weak as any other man," he said.

While the Philistines hid in the next room, Delilah playfully tied Samson up with seven new bowstrings. "Help!" she cried. "The Philistines are upon us!"

Samson leapt up, easily breaking free from the bowstrings.

Delilah was upset. "Why did you mock me and lie to me? You have made me look like a fool," she said to Samson. "Please tell me the truth now—how can someone capture you?"

Samson then told Delilah that he could only be captured if he was tied up with ropes that had never been used before.

Delilah quickly tied Samson up with new ropes. But when she called out that the Philistines were upon him, Samson snapped the new ropes as if they were threads.

"Again you have made me look like a fool!" said Delilah. "Please tell me truly how you might be captured."

"Weave locks of my long hair into the cloth on your loom," Samson said. "Then I will lose all my strength."

Samson fell asleep, and Delilah wove his long hair into the cloth on her loom. But once again, she cried out, "The Philistines are upon us!" And again Samson broke free.

Delilah wept bitterly. "If you love me," she said, "you will stop lying and tell me your secret."

Delilah's persistence had finally worn Samson down. "I will tell you the truth," he said. "My strength is in my hair. If my hair is cut with a razor, I will become as weak as any other man."

Exhausted, Samson then fell asleep with his head in Delilah's lap.

Delilah motioned to the Philistines. One of them crept in and silently cut off Samson's long hair. When he was done, Delilah let out a piercing shriek. "Wake up, Samson!" she cried. "The Philistines are attacking us!"

Samson leapt to his feet. He was bewildered to find that he was no stronger than other men.

Quickly the Philistines overpowered Samson. They held him down and gouged out his eyes. Then they dragged Samson to prison in Gaza and shackled him with bronze chains. Blind, imprisoned, and alone, Samson was forced to grind wheat for his captors. But as time passed, no one noticed that Samson's hair had begun to grow again.

The rulers of the Philistines gave credit to their god Dagon for defeating Samson, so they planned a big celebration at Dagon's temple to celebrate his victory.

On the day of the festival, the temple was crowded with people. All the rulers of the Philistines arrived with great fanfare. Everyone was singing, laughing, and drinking. The temple became so crowded that three thousand Philistines climbed up on the roof to enjoy the celebration. Finally, someone shouted, "Bring Samson out to entertain us!"

A boy servant led Samson into the hall of the temple, holding his hand to guide him. The once powerful man was now a pitiful sight. The Philistines jeered and made fun of Samson as he shuffled in, blind and chained.

Samson asked the boy to lead him to the two main pillars of the temple, so he might feel them with his hands and lean against them. Putting his arms around the pillars, Samson

prayed, "Lord God, I cannot see, for the Philistines have put out my eyes. Let me pay them back. Please give me strength one more time."

Slowly Samson leaned on the pillars with all his might. There was a huge roar and the pillars came thundering down, bringing the temple with it! No one escaped. Along with Samson, all the Philistines at the celebration died.

God's plan for Samson was complete. His grieving brothers brought his body home, and they buried him in the tomb of his father, Manoah.

Loyal Ruth

(Ruth 1–4)

or a long time, no rain fell in the land of the Israelites and no crops grew. Many Israelites were forced to move to the land of Moab, where there was plenty of food. Among them were a man named Elimelech; his wife, Naomi; and their two sons. When Elimelech died, his sons married two Moabite women named Ruth and Orpah. For the next ten years, Naomi lived happily with her sons and their wives in Moab. Then, sadly, Naomi's two sons also died.

When Naomi was left without her husband or her sons, she decided to go back home to the land of Judah. The wives of her two sons prepared to travel with her, and the three of them started back to Judah. But on the way, Naomi stopped her two daughters-in-law.

"You should go back to your own mothers now. May the Lord deal kindly with you," Naomi said, "for you need to find new husbands in your own land. You do not need to be tied to me, for I have no more sons to give you."

Both women clung to Naomi and wept, for they loved her

dearly. Reluctantly, Orpah left her mother-in-law and returned to her own people, but Ruth refused to leave Naomi.

"Please do not ask me to go," Ruth begged Naomi. "Wherever you go, I will go. Your people will be my people. Your God will be my God. Wherever you die, there I will die and be buried. Only death can separate me from you."

When Naomi saw how her daughter-in-law loved her, she said that Ruth could come with her. Then the two women set off together on their long journey to Naomi's home.

It was harvesttime when Naomi and Ruth arrived in Bethlehem, and people were hard at work in the fields. When Naomi's relatives and friends saw her, they rushed to greet her.

Ruth saw that there was barley left in the field. She asked Naomi if she could gather some of it. A cousin of Naomi's named Boaz was working nearby, and he noticed Ruth and asked her name. Later Boaz was very moved to hear about Ruth's loyalty to Naomi, and he invited Ruth to come and eat with him.

One night Naomi called Ruth to her. "Boaz will be winnowing barley on the threshing floor tonight," Naomi said. "After he falls asleep, lie down at his feet."

Ruth did as Naomi told her. She lay down at Boaz's feet. Boaz woke with a start and saw Ruth lying nearby.

"Who are you?" he asked.

"I am Ruth, your servant," she said. "Please spread your cloak over me. I wish you to take care of me."

Boaz met with ten of the city's elders, and he asked them to witness his promise to marry Ruth and take care of Naomi. His wish was granted.

To Naomi's joy, Ruth and Boaz married. Soon they had a baby son. Naomi was overwhelmed with joy. As she held the tiny boy in her arms, she knew that God had sent him as a gift to her and her faithful daughter-in-law, Ruth. All the women said to Naomi, "Blessed be the Lord, who has not left you this day without next of kin." They named the baby Obed, and he became the father of Jesse and the grandfather of David.

Young Samuel Serves God
(1 Samuel 1–3)

woman named Hannah was happily married to a good man. But both of them were very sorrowful about one thing—they had never had a child.

One day Hannah and her husband took offerings to the tabernacle of Shiloh. "Dear God," Hannah prayed, "please send us a son. If you do, I promise we will give him back to you, and he will serve you all his life." Eli the priest saw Hannah praying, and when he approached her, Hannah confided to him that she desperately yearned for a child.

"Go in peace," the priest said warmly, "and may God grant your request."

Hannah left the tabernacle with a joyful heart, and in less than a year, she gave birth to a baby boy. She named him Samuel, which means "God heard," for God had heard her prayers.

When Samuel was a young boy, Hannah packed his clothes in a small satchel. Then she journeyed with Samuel to the temple of the Lord in Shiloh. Hannah also took along a young bull, a container of wine, and some flour to give as an offering.

Eli the priest greeted Hannah and Samuel at the door of the temple.

"Do you remember me?" said Hannah. "I am the woman who asked God for a child. He answered my prayers, and now I have come to give the boy back to God for as long as the child lives."

Samuel stayed at the temple and served Eli. Every year Hannah and her husband came to visit their son. They always brought him a coat that Hannah had made and other presents as well. Hannah eventually had more children, but Samuel always remained close to her heart.

Eli had two sons who were also priests. Greedy and sly, Eli's sons often stole the offerings meant for God. Although Eli knew that his two sons were wicked, he allowed them to work in the temple.

One night, when he was still a boy, Samuel awoke from a sound sleep to hear a voice calling out "Samuel! Samuel!" Believing that Eli was calling him, the boy ran to the bedside of the priest.

"I did not call you, Samuel," Eli said. "Go back to bed."

Again the voice called out to Samuel. And again Samuel rushed to Eli's bed. Once more Eli reassured the boy it was not he who had called.

After God had called Samuel a third time, Eli understood that God must be speaking directly to Samuel.

"Go back to your bed, Samuel," Eli said quietly. "But this time when you hear a voice, say, 'Speak to me, God. Your servant is listening.'"

Samuel did as he was told. God told him that he was going to punish Eli's wicked sons. And Eli, too, would be punished for ignoring their evil ways.

The next morning, Samuel went into Eli's room. Eli was old and almost blind. Samuel sadly told him what God had said. When he had finished, Eli said, "This is the will of God. It must be as he says."

The Ark Is Captured

(1 Samuel 4–6)

The Philistines and the Israelites remained bitter enemies. In one battle with the Philistines, the Israelites lost over four thousand men. Afterward, when the survivors straggled back to their camp, their leaders met to discuss their terrible defeat.

"Let us get the Ark from the Tabernacle in Shiloh. Then we can actually take God among us into battle, and God will save us from the power of our enemies," someone said.

Soldiers of the Israelites journeyed to Shiloh and brought back the Ark of the Covenant, the golden box that held the tablets with the Ten Commandments. When the precious Ark arrived in the camp of the Israelites, all of Israel shouted with joy.

The Philistine soldiers wondered what the celebration was about. When they discovered that the Israelites had the Ark, they grew afraid. "Be brave, Philistines!" their leaders urged. "Fight like men, or you will become slaves of the Israelites as they have been to you!"

The Philistines fought fiercely and won the great battle. Thirty thousand Israelite soldiers were slain, including Eli's two sons. But worst of all, the Philistines captured the Ark of the Covenant.

A soldier from the tribe of Benjamin rushed back to Shiloh with the terrible news. When he arrived, Eli the priest was sitting at the gate by the road. He was desperate for news of the Ark. When the old, blind priest heard the cries of his people, he asked what had happened.

"Israel has fled from the Philistines!" the messenger said. "Your sons are dead, and the Ark of the Covenant has been stolen!"

Overcome with agony, Eli fell off his chair. He broke his neck and died.

Stealing the Ark soon brought disaster to the Philistines. They set the Ark up next to their idol Dagon in his temple at Ashdod. In the morning, the statue of Dagon lay on the ground before the Ark. The people put Dagon back in his place. But the following day, the priests found Dagon on the ground again. Only this time his head and hands were missing. Soon all the people in Ashdod woke to find painful sores covering their flesh.

Blaming their woes on the stolen Ark, the Philistines were desperate to be rid of it. They gathered together to find a solution. They decided that once they sent the Ark away, their problems would be over. But every place where the Ark of the Covenant was set up, the people were soon beset with troubles.

Finally, the Philistines decided to test the power of the God of the Israelites. They placed the Ark in a cart pulled by two untrained oxen. The oxen trudged away down the road.

Later, the Israelites were working in their wheat fields when someone spotted oxen slowly pulling a cart. As the oxen came closer, the Israelites couldn't believe their eyes. They saw that the cart held the Ark of the Covenant.

With great care, the Israelites lifted the sacred box out of the cart and lowered it to the ground. Then they rejoiced, thanking God for safely returning their beloved Ark.

King Saul

(1 Samuel 8–12)

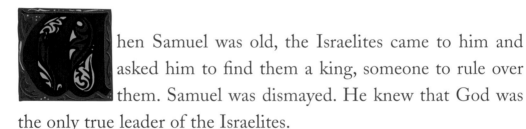

hen Samuel was old, the Israelites came to him and asked him to find them a king, someone to rule over them. Samuel was dismayed. He knew that God was the only true leader of the Israelites.

Samuel turned to God for help. God said, "The people are wrong to put a king in my place. Warn them that a king can take away their freedom."

Samuel gave God's message to the Israelites, but they still demanded a king to rule over them and take care of them. Samuel spoke with God again, and this time God told him to choose a man named Saul from the tribe of Benjamin.

A short time later, as Samuel was walking out of the city gates, a tall young man approached him.

"Here is the man of whom I spoke," God said to Samuel. "He is the one who shall rule over my people."

"I have come to see a prophet in your city," Saul said. "I am searching for my father's lost donkeys. I was hoping the prophet could help me find them."

"I am the prophet you seek," Samuel told Saul, "and the animals you seek have been found. Come and spend the night at my house, for there are important things we must discuss. You are going to be the first king of the Israelites."

Saul was shocked. "Can this be possible? My tribe is the smallest tribe in Israel, and my family is the smallest family in the tribe," he said. "I am not powerful enough to be king!"

But Samuel told Saul that he must come with him, and he led the young man to a feast at his house.

Thirty guests had arrived, but Samuel saved the choicest food for Saul. After dinner he and Saul went to a secluded spot to talk. Early the next morning, as Saul left, Samuel took out a vial of oil and poured it over Saul's head and kissed him.

"The Lord has anointed you ruler over his people," Samuel said. "When you leave the city, a group of prophets will greet you. They will be singing and playing the harp, tambourine, flute, and lyre and praising God. The spirit of God will enter you, and God will help make you a changed man."

Samuel called all the tribes of Israel together at Mizpah. He announced that soon they would know who their king was to be. Samuel told the tribe of Benjamin to pass by in family groups. When Saul's family came forward, Saul was missing. God told them where he was hiding.

Saul was soon found and brought out from his hiding place. Everyone gasped to see the tall young man standing before them.

"Do you see the one whom the Lord has chosen?" said Samuel. "There is no one else like him."

Saul returned home and continued to live a quiet life on his father's farm. He was working in the fields one day when he heard a great clamor. Messengers had arrived with the news that Nahash, the cruel king of the Ammonites, had attacked the Israelite towns of Jabesh and Gilead. The towns had offered to make a treaty with him, but he refused, saying that he would accept their surrender only after he had gouged out the right eye of every man there.

Saul hastened to raise an army. He had all the oxen he owned slaughtered and cut into tiny pieces. Then he gave the pieces to his men, who rushed to all the Israelite towns carrying the pieces with them. Their message was terrifying: If you do not gather to fight the Ammonites, this will be the fate of all your animals!

Three hundred and seventy thousand soldiers from Israel and Judah hastened to join Saul. As they prepared for battle, Saul divided them into three divisions. At dawn the next day, the Israelites attacked. The Israelites fought well, and by noon they were victorious.

As the Israelites celebrated, Samuel spoke to them: "Your king now walks before you. If you and your king fear God and serve him, all will be well. But if you do not listen to the voice of God, then God will be against you and your king. Now see this thing that God will do before your eyes. He will send thunder and rain."

Then Samuel called upon God, and God sent thunder and rain to show that all Samuel had said was true.

Saul Displeases God
(1 Samuel 13–16)

The Israelites' old enemy, the Philistines, continued to threaten them. One day they massed on the Israelites' borders and prepared to attack. The Philistines had well-trained, powerful soldiers and over three thousand chariots, six thousand horsemen, and a multitude of troops. The Israelites were fearful and hid in caves, holes, and tombs.

Samuel assured Saul that he would soon come to offer sacrifices to God, so that God would be with Saul's army. But Samuel delayed his trip for several days, and in that time, Saul grew very anxious. The soldiers sensed their king's fear and began to desert the army.

As his forces dwindled, Saul grew more and more desperate. Finally, he went to the altar to make a burnt offering.

Samuel arrived just as smoke was rising from the altar. "You have broken the laws of God!" Samuel said angrily to Saul. "You know that only priests and Levites can light the altar fires. No one who disobeys God can prevail as king. Your descendants will not rule over Israel! God will choose another who is more faithful to his word."

After Samuel said these words, Saul and his army were victorious over the Philistines. But the king's relationship with God was broken forever.

Saul kept disobeying God. But the more he relied on his own power rather than God's, the weaker he became. Samuel spent many nights weeping and praying for King Saul. Then he decided to meet with him.

Saul begged Samuel for God's forgiveness and asked Samuel to stand by him. But Samuel was unyielding, and as he rose to leave, Saul clutched at Samuel's robe, ripping the cloth. Slowly Samuel turned to face him. "The Lord has torn your kingdom from you just as you have torn my garment. He has given it to a neighbor of yours, who is better than you," he said.

Later Samuel thought deeply about who should rule over the Israelites. One day God commanded Samuel to travel to Bethlehem. "When you get there, search for a man named Jesse. His son will be the next king of the Israelites."

Samuel's arrival created a stir in Bethlehem, and the elders of the city trembled when they met him. No one knew why this powerful man was visiting their town. With great reverence, everyone lined up for Samuel's blessing.

Seven of Jesse's sons waited to see Samuel. Even though they were all handsome, God had warned Samuel about judging a person by his looks alone. "Men look at the outer appearance," God said, "but I look into the heart."

Samuel asked if all of Jesse's children were present. He was told that only David, the youngest, was missing, for he was out in the fields tending sheep.

"Send for David," said Samuel. "We will not sit down until he arrives."

David was summoned, and when he came in from the fields, Samuel saw that the young man had beautiful eyes and was tanned and strong from living outdoors. But Samuel could also see into David's heart, and he saw that he was good.

"Rise and anoint him, for he is the one," God said to Samuel.

Samuel took out a vial of oil and asked David to kneel down. Then Samuel anointed him with the oil, and from then on, David was filled with the spirit of God.

When Samuel left Bethlehem to begin his journey to Ramah, his mind was peaceful. He knew God had chosen the right man.

David and Goliath

(1 Samuel 17–18)

Some time later, the Philistine army gathered to strike against Israel. Soldiers camped on top of a hill and prepared for battle against the Israelites. Saul and his men took up a position on a hill across the valley of Elah.

The Israelites waited nervously for the battle to begin. But to their amazement, a huge champion fighter named Goliath strode out of the Philistines' camp. The Israelites had never seen anyone like him before. Goliath was over nine feet tall! A bronze helmet covered his massive head. He wore a heavy coat of armor, and his huge legs were encased in bronze.

The giant stood with his feet planted on the ground. His weapons gleamed harshly in the sunlight. A javelin of bronze hung from his back, and in his hands, he held another spear whose blade alone weighed fifteen pounds.

"Am I not a Philistine and are you not the servants of Saul?" he thundered. "I dare you to settle this battle by sending one of your men out to fight me! If I win, you will become our servants! If *he* wins, we will serve you!"

Saul and the Israelites were terrified. They knew that none of them could defeat a giant of such great strength. Every morning and every evening for forty days, Goliath strode out into the open and bellowed his challenge. As each day passed, the Israelites became more fearful.

Three of David's brothers served in Saul's army. One morning David's father asked him to take provisions to them. David left home carrying grain, bread, and cheese to give his brothers and their commanders. He arrived at the battlefield just as Goliath was delivering his terrible message.

When David saw the terror on the faces of the Israelite soldiers, he could not help himself. "*I* will kill this man!" he shouted.

The soldiers were startled by David's words, and David's brothers were angry. They could not imagine how their youngest brother could defeat this giant.

When Saul sent for David, the young man insisted he was the king's servant. "I will fight this Philistine for you!" said David. "I have killed a lion and a bear to protect my sheep. Surely I can kill this man who stands against the armies of the living God. The God who saved me from the paw of the lion and from the paw of the bear will save me from the hand of this Philistine."

"Go then," said Saul, "and may God be with you."

Saul dressed David in his own helmet and armor. But David took them off, for he wanted to wear his simple shepherd's clothing instead. As everyone watched, David walked to a nearby stream. Bending down, he carefully chose five smooth stones. He tucked the stones into his shepherd's pouch and picked up his sling. Then he strode forward to face the giant.

Goliath was outraged to see such a young man approach him. He thought the Israelites were making fun of him. "Why are you

sending this child to fight me?" he roared. "Am I a dog that you can defeat with a stick?"

David stared up at him. "You come to me with sword and spear and javelin," he said. "I come to you with my God!"

As Goliath strode forward, David took a stone from his pouch and put it into his sling. Then he aimed the stone straight at Goliath. It hit him in the forehead.

Goliath reeled. Then, with a terrible crash, he fell face-forward onto the ground. David had killed the mighty giant with only one small stone. David then lifted the giant's mighty sword and cut off his head.

In terror, the Philistines ran from the battlefield. The Israelites chased after them, killing and wounding a great number.

As the Israelites celebrated their victory, Saul called for David. "Who are you?" he asked.

"I am David," the young man answered, "the son of Jesse of Bethlehem."

On that day, King Saul took David into his own home to live with his family. The king's daughter Michal soon fell in love with David; and the king's son Jonathan became David's best friend.

Saul Turns Against David

(1 Samuel 18–31)

After David's victory, Saul made him commander of his warriors. Whenever David led men into battle, he was victorious, because God was with him. All the people, even the servants of Saul, came to love the young man.

Everywhere David went, people gathered to sing his praises. One day, as he was returning home after another victory over the Philistines, women ran out and danced around him, playing their tambourines. They sang:

"Saul has slain his thousands,
And David his ten thousands."

Saul was overcome with anger and jealousy. He brooded so much about David's fame that his heart grew cold. The next night, as David played his lyre for Saul, a fury seized the king. Twice he threw his spear at David. Each time, David escaped unhurt.

Saul feared that God was with David and no longer with him. His hatred for David grew so strong that he plotted to put David in grave danger, hoping he would be killed. Saul promised to give David his daughter Michal in marriage if he killed one hundred Philistines. To the king's dismay, David killed twice that number, and again the people celebrated him as a great hero.

Saul was more determined than ever to kill him. The king's son Jonathan warned David to go into hiding.

"Why do you want to slay the innocent for no reason?" he asked his father.

After Jonathan spoke to Saul, the king felt so remorseful he allowed Jonathan to bring David back to his house. But when war broke out again and David won, jealousy overtook Saul once more. Angrily Saul hurled his spear at David while he was playing his beautiful music.

David hurried to the house where he lived with Michal. She warned him that he must flee that very night, or he would die the next day. When Saul's men came to kill him, Michal lowered David from a window, and he escaped. Michal then put goat's hair on a statue, and placed it in their bed to fool the soldiers.

David sought refuge in the country, joining Samuel in Ramah. Jonathan promised to give David a sign on the day after the new moon to let him know when he could safely return.

When that day came, David hid behind some rocks, waiting for Jonathan to signal whether it was safe for him to return. When Jonathan signaled that it was not, David rose and hurried to him. The two men kissed each other and wept. "Go in peace," said Jonathan, "for God will always be between your descendants and my descendants." Then David and Jonathan parted in sorrow.

David found shelter in a cave. Friends heard about his plight and hurried to him. Their number grew until David became captain of about four hundred fighting men.

One day Saul and three thousand of his men went to the desert in search of David. The sun was blazing hot, and Saul took refuge in a cool cave. He didn't know that David and some of his followers were hiding deep within the cave.

While Saul rested, David crept up silently behind him and snipped off a corner of Saul's cloak. When Saul left the cave, he heard a voice ring out, "My lord the king!"

Saul turned around and was astonished to see David standing at the mouth of the cave. David bowed before Saul and said, "Why do you listen to people who say I am going to harm you? If I wanted to hurt you, I would have done so today. Look! A piece of your cloak is in my hand! I could have easily killed you. Whom are you after? A dead dog? A flea?"

Saul wept with guilt and remorse. "You are a more righteous man than I, David," he said. "Surely you will rule Israel someday. Swear that you will not kill my descendants and that you will not destroy my name."

David gave this promise to Saul. Then the two men parted. When Saul returned home, David went back into hiding. David knew that Saul's remorse would not last.

In the days that followed, Samuel died. All the Israelites gathered to mourn the wise prophet. Without Samuel, Saul grew even more fearful and angry. He believed that everyone was plotting against him. When Philistine armies threatened the Israelites again, Saul was afraid and prayed fervently, but God did not listen.

Saul was in such despair that he decided to visit the Witch of Endor, who told the future. That night, he disguised himself and went to see her. Saul begged the witch to call forth Samuel from the dead.

The witch went into a trance. From out of the depths, she summoned up an old man wrapped in a robe. Instantly Saul recognized him as Samuel.

"Why have you disturbed me by bringing me up?" Samuel asked.

"I am in great distress, for God has turned away from me," said Saul.

"Since you have disobeyed God, you will lose your kingdom. The Philistines will be victorious. Tomorrow you and your sons shall die!" replied Samuel.

At these words, Saul fell on the ground in terror. The witch gave Saul food to restore his strength. Then he left her and went out into the night.

Samuel's words came true. The next day, thousands of Israelite soldiers, including Jonathan and his brothers, died in the bloody slaughter. Saul was mortally wounded, and begged his armor bearer to drive a sword through him, but the young man refused. Saul fell on his own sword and died.

The people of Jabesh remembered how Saul had saved them so long ago. To honor him, they buried the bones of the king and his three sons under the tamarisk tree of Jabesh, and then they fasted for seven days.

David the King

(2 Samuel 1–6)

avid received the news about the deaths of his beloved friend Jonathan and King Saul. David wrote a long song in which he praised both Saul and Jonathan, saying:

"They were swifter than eagles.
They were stronger than lions."

Then David asked God what to do, and God told him to go back to the land of Judah and live in Hebron.

The men of Judah came to Hebron and rejoiced that David was their new leader. After he had been anointed as king, David drove the Philistines out of the land of the Israelites and made Jerusalem the capital city.

One day King David and thirty thousand followers set out to bring the Ark of the Covenant to Jerusalem. After carefully loading the Ark onto a cart, they started their journey. Walking alongside the cart, David and others sang and played harps, lyres, castanets, tambourines, and cymbals.

As the Ark moved down the road, it started to slip off the cart. One of the men reached out his hand to steady it. As soon as the man touched the Ark, God struck him dead. This frightened David so much he left it in the hands of Obed-edom, the priest, for three months.

Finally, David went back to get the Ark and asked the priests to carry it on to Jerusalem. After the Ark passed through the city gates, the air was filled with the joyous sound of trumpets. Everyone danced and sang.

King David himself shook off his robes and danced around the sacred Ark, leaping wildly and whirling in circles. As evening fell, he passed out bread and dates and raisin cake to the revelers. By the end of the day, David began plans to build a temple in Jerusalem.

David's wife Michal was angry when she saw his leaping and dancing. She complained to him that he should not have danced before the Ark like a barbarian.

"Today was a celebration for God," King David said. "God chose me over your father. I will feel free the rest of my life to dance in honor of God."

Wise King Solomon

(1 Kings 1–8)

After ruling Israel for forty years, David knew his end was near. As he grew weaker, he called for his favorite son, Solomon, one last time. "I will die soon," David said. "Be strong and courageous. Always walk with God and keep his commandments." David was buried in the City of David, where he rested with his ancestors. Even though David did not always follow God's laws, he had ruled well, and his kingdom was strong and secure.

Solomon became the king of the Israelites. He did not crave power and fame. Indeed, he was so humble that he did not know whether he could ever become a good ruler.

To ease his mind, Solomon went to Gibeon and offered God a thousand burnt offerings. That night he had a dream, and in his dream, he spoke to God: "Please give me a heart to understand the people," he prayed, "and help me know the difference between good and evil, and help me be a wise leader."

It pleased God that Solomon had not asked him for riches or for the death of his enemies. So God

answered him in the dream, saying, "I shall give you a wise heart, and since you did not ask for riches and glory, I shall give you those, too. And I shall give you a long life if you follow my laws and commandments."

Soon after, two women came to him for his judgment. Both shared the same house, and each had recently given birth to a boy child. Sadly, one baby had died, while the other had lived. Now each woman claimed the living child as her own.

Solomon listened carefully as the two women argued. Then he said, "Bring me a sword." And a servant brought him a sword.

"We will use the sword to cut the baby in half," said King Solomon. "Then each of you will get half of a child."

One of the women rushed forward and fell on her knees. "Oh, my lord, give her the baby," she sobbed. "Please do not kill him!"

But the other woman agreed that Solomon should give each of them half of the baby. "Then it will be neither mine nor hers!" she said.

Now Solomon knew the truth. He knew who the real mother was. "Give the baby to the first woman," he ordered.

Word of Solomon's wise decision traveled all over Israel. The people realized God had given him great wisdom and they stood in awe of him.

To carry out his father's wish, Solomon began building a beautiful temple for God. It took seven years to complete. Then he decided to bring the Ark of the Covenant to rest there.

Walking in front of a

procession of priests, Solomon escorted the Ark to the temple. Suddenly a cloud filled with the presence of God engulfed the room.

Then Solomon stood in front of everyone. He lifted his voice in praise and thanksgiving. "The Lord has said that he would dwell in thick darkness. Lord, I have built an exalted house, a place for you to dwell in forever."

Finally, King Solomon implored the Israelites to keep their hearts true to God and always walk in God's ways.

Elijah and the Prophets of Baal

(1 Kings 11–18)

After many years of peaceful rule, King Solomon died. Unfortunately, his son was a spoiled young man with little of his father's wisdom. Under his rule, the country fell into disorder and chaos. People turned away from God and went back to the worship of golden calves.

But one man knew the truth and was prepared to risk his life to tell it. He was a prophet named Elijah. One day Elijah decided to visit King Ahab, who was then the king of the Israelites. King Ahab was more wicked than all the kings before him. He had erected an altar and a sacred pole to worship the idol of Baal, a false god.

"By the power of the God of Israel, the God whom I serve, there will be no rain or dew in the coming years," Elijah warned King Ahab. "They will only return when I give the word."

For three years, the severe drought persisted in the land of the Israelites. Fields dried to hard-baked earth, crops withered, and people and animals died of hunger and thirst. Finally, the word of the Lord directed Elijah to visit King Ahab once again.

When Elijah appeared, the king looked angrily at him. "Are you the one who is causing so much trouble?" he said.

"It is not I who created the drought," Elijah replied. "You have forsaken God's commandments. You are worshipping the idol Baal and ignoring God. Gather your people together and bring them to the top of Mount Carmel. Bring your prophets as well."

King Ahab was so desperate that he agreed. He led the Israelites and four hundred and fifty prophets of Baal to the top of Mount Carmel.

Elijah looked out over the crowd. "You cannot serve both Baal and God," he said sternly. "You must choose one over the other."

Elijah ordered the prophets of Baal to build an altar for their god, while he built an altar to the God of the Israelites. As the priests of Baal set to work, Elijah had two young bulls killed and cut into pieces. He then divided the pieces between the two altars.

"Don't light the fire under the offerings," he told the prophets. "Call upon your god and I will call upon mine. Whichever god answers by fire is the true god."

The prophets called out to their idol. "Oh, Baal, answer us!"

But there was no answer.

All morning the prophets shouted and pleaded and hobbled around their altar.

At noon Elijah mocked them. "Call louder to your god!" he said. "Perhaps he is away on a journey. Perhaps he is asleep and needs to be woken up!"

As midday passed, the prophets raved on. They cut themselves with swords and spears until their blood flowed. But still there was no answer from Baal. Help did not come to them.

Finally, Elijah walked slowly to his altar. He asked for buckets of water and poured it on the wood. Everyone was puzzled, for wet

wood could not burn. But Elijah began to pray. "O God, let it be known that you are the God of Israel," he said. "Answer me, Lord, so that these people will follow the true God."

Suddenly the wet altar was consumed in flames! The fire burned the offering, the wood, the stones, and the dust. It licked up the water that had collected in ditches around the altar. Everything burned to ashes.

The people fell to the ground. "The Lord is indeed God!" they cried. "The Lord is indeed God!"

Elijah walked to the top of Mount Carmel and bowed down. "Go and look toward the sea," he said to his servant. The man looked and saw nothing.

Elijah kept telling the servant to look. "Go again, seven more times," he said. The seventh time, the servant finally saw something.

"I see a small cloud," he said, "rising from the sea."

"Go tell King Ahab to harness his chariots and return home, for if he does not leave at once, the rains will stop him," Elijah said.

Soon black clouds covered the sky, the wind began to blow hard, and a heavy rain started to fall. Elijah tightened his garments around him and hurried down the mountainside.

The terrible drought had finally come to an end.

Elijah and the Chariot of Fire

(2 Kings 2)

After many years had passed, Elijah knew he would soon die and be taken up to heaven by a whirlwind. He had worked hard to keep the Israelites on the right path, but now his time on earth was coming to an end.

God chose a man named Elisha to become the next great prophet after Elijah. Elisha had been with Elijah for some time and loved him dearly.

One day the two men set out on their last journey together. Several times Elijah asked Elisha to leave him so he could travel alone. But Elisha did not want to part from his friend. "As the Lord lives, and as you yourself live, I will not leave you," he told Elijah.

When the two came to the river Jordan, Elijah took off his coat. He rolled it up and struck the water with it. The waters parted, and the two men walked across a dry path. When they reached the other side of the river, Elijah asked Elisha what he could do for him before he died.

"Please leave me a double share of your spirit," Elisha said.

"You have asked a hard thing. But if you can see me when I leave you, it will be yours," Elijah said mysteriously.

As they continued walking and talking, a chariot of fire and two horses of fire suddenly appeared and separated the two men. A whirlwind lifted Elijah and the chariot slowly up to heaven.

For a moment Elisha lost sight of Elijah in the whirlwind. Then he caught sight of him one last time. As the chariot disappeared deeper into the whirlwind, Elisha kept watching. "My father! My father!" he cried out. When he could no longer see Elijah, he grasped his clothes and tore them in two pieces.

Then Elisha picked up Elijah's coat from the ground. He struck the river Jordan with the coat, and a path appeared through the water. As Elisha crossed safely back to the other side of the river, he knew that the spirit of Elijah was alive within him.

Daniel and the Lions' Den
(Daniel 1, 6)

In the years after Elijah's death, Israel fought off many invaders. Finally, a powerful nation called Babylonia attacked Jerusalem and carried some of the Israelites into captivity. Among the captured Israelites was one named Daniel, a man of great wisdom and courage.

The king of Babylonia recognized Daniel's many gifts. He trusted him and granted him great power. But when Daniel became the second most important man in Babylonia, others in the court were consumed with jealousy. They plotted against him. They knew the only way to destroy Daniel was to force him to break the laws of God.

One day Daniel's enemies went to King Darius with a wicked plan. They told the king to issue a decree stating that for one month no one but King Darius could pray to any god—anyone who disobeyed this law would be put to death.

The king did as the men requested. Because of his faith, Daniel continued to pray to God three times a day. As it was his habit to pray in front of an open window facing Jerusalem, people on the street could easily see him.

Someone soon reported Daniel's disobedience to King Darius, and the king was forced to give the order that Daniel should be put to death. Daniel's enemies grabbed him and threw him into a den filled with hungry lions. There was no escape.

Saddened by Daniel's terrible fate, King Darius made every effort to rescue him, but to no avail. Hoping God might have mercy on Daniel, the king fasted throughout the night. When dawn came, he rushed to the lions' den, dreading to see what had happened to Daniel during the night.

"Daniel, are you still alive?" the king called. "Has your God helped and delivered you?"

Daniel answered from the lions' den, "My God sent angels to protect me, for I am innocent. I never did anything to hurt you, my king."

Darius was filled with joy. Immediately he called for Daniel's release. Then King Darius punished the evil men who had plotted against Daniel. They and their wives and their children were all thrown into the den of the savage lions. This time there was no angel for protection. The lions ate them up as soon as their feet touched the floor of the den. Only their bones remained.

Jonah and the Giant Fish

(Jonah 1–4)

ineveh was the great capital city of a country called Assyria. When God became unhappy with the people of Nineveh, he called on a prophet named Jonah.

"Go to Nineveh," God ordered Jonah. "There is much evil in that city. You must go and cry out against it."

But Jonah did not want to go. He decided to run away from God. Instead of going to Nineveh, he paid his fare and climbed aboard a boat in Joppa and sailed toward the city of Tarshish.

God knew that Jonah was disobeying him. He sent a terrible storm out over the sea, and the boat rocked violently in the raging winds.

The sailors were terrified. They dropped to their knees and prayed to their own gods. Then they threw their cargo into the sea to lighten the ship's load.

Jonah was asleep in his cabin. The captain stumbled below and woke him up. "Why are you sleeping?" he said. "You also need to pray to your god so that we don't die!"

As the storm raged on, the sailors grew more desperate. They cast lots to discover who had brought such trouble upon their ship. The lot fell on Jonah, showing that he was the guilty man. The sailors hurried below and angrily confronted him. "What shall we do to you so the sea may quiet down?"

"Yes, I have caused this trouble," confessed Jonah. "I am an Israelite who is running away from God. Pick me up and throw me into the sea; then the sea will quiet down for you."

When the storm worsened and the waves towered above the small boat, the frantic sailors threw Jonah overboard. The waters grew calm, and the storm ceased.

As Jonah struggled to stay afloat, a giant fish appeared and swallowed him whole. Jonah stayed in its stomach for three days and nights.

While Jonah was inside the belly of the large fish, he prayed to God:

"So I called to the Lord and he answered me.
I was about to die, so I cried to you,
And you heard my voice. . . .
The deep sea was all around me.
Seaweed was wrapped around my head.
But you saved me from death,
Lord my God."

After three days, God spoke to the fish, and it threw Jonah out of its mouth onto dry land. Once again God ordered Jonah to Nineveh. And this time, Jonah obeyed.

Jonah's powerful prophecy had a great effect on the people who heard him. After they promised to worship the Lord, God spared them from harm.

The Return from Captivity

(Ezra and Nehemiah)

Finally, after many long years of captivity in Babylon, in the first year of King Cyrus of Persia, the Israelites were allowed to return home. As they straggled into Jerusalem, they saw destruction everywhere. The city walls had been reduced to rubble, and the houses were in ruins.

Most of the returning Israelites had never known the old Jerusalem, but now they all agreed that it must be rebuilt. Where should they start? How could they ever help Jerusalem recover its ancient beauty?

The answer finally came from an Israelite named Nehemiah who served the new king of Persia. One day the king saw that Nehemiah looked unhappy. "Why are you so downcast?" the king asked him.

"My heart is broken," replied Nehemiah. "Jerusalem, the beloved home of my people, is in ruins. I wish I could be there to help them rebuild the city."

The king gave Nehemiah permission to leave. He sent him home with armed guards and letters for the local officials.

When Nehemiah arrived in Jerusalem, he found the city in

great disorder. But soon he began organizing its reconstruction. As Nehemiah directed the builders, many doubters stood near the work sites and jeered. But Nehemiah armed his men with weapons to keep away the troublemakers.

In fifty-two days, the wall of Jerusalem was standing once again. Earlier, in the rubble of the city, someone had found the remains of the ancient temple. A few stones even remained from the old altar. New stones were gathered to rebuild the altar. And in the morning and in the evening, the priests again lit fires and made offerings to God, just as their ancestors had done.

In the seventh month, the people of Israel gathered in the square by the Water Gate. They asked Ezra, a teacher, to bring out the Book of the Teachings of Moses. Ezra stood on a high wooden platform built for the occasion and read aloud from early morning until noon.

When Ezra praised God, all the people lifted up their hands and shouted, "Amen! Amen!" Then they bowed down and worshipped the Lord, their God.

An Angel Brings News to Mary

(Luke 1)

A young woman named Mary lived in the town of Nazareth in Galilee. Mary was engaged to marry Joseph, a carpenter, who was descended from the house of David. One day God sent the angel Gabriel to visit Mary.

Mary was alone when the angel appeared before her. "Greetings, favored one," he said to her, "the Lord is with you."

Mary was confused and frightened. She struggled to understand what the angel's words meant. "Do not be afraid, Mary," he said, "for you have found favor with God. You will conceive and bear a child whose name will be Jesus."

"But how can this be," Mary asked, "since I do not have a husband?"

"The Holy Spirit will come upon you," the angel said. "The power of the Most High will overshadow you, and the child born to you will be the Holy Son of God."

Mary was stunned by these words, but she consented to God's will and said, "I am a servant of the Lord. Let everything happen as you have said." Then the angel departed from her.

The Birth of Jesus

(Matthew 1–2, Luke 2)

Soon after Joseph and Mary were married, an order came down from the Roman emperor Augustus for all people to return to their birthplace so that they could be counted and taxed. Although Mary's child was soon to be born, Joseph and Mary began the long journey south to Bethlehem in Judea, the birthplace of Joseph's family.

The city was crowded and there were no rooms in the inn. Mary and Joseph had to sleep in a stable. While they were there, the baby was born. Mary wrapped him in swaddling clothes and laid him in the manger.

Shepherds were keeping watch over their flocks in the fields nearby. An angel suddenly appeared before them at night. The glory of the Lord shone all around the angel, and the shepherds were filled with fear.

The angel said, "Do not be afraid. I bring good news of great joy for all people. Unto you is born a savior, who is Christ the Lord. You shall find him in Bethlehem, lying in a manger."

A multitude of angels then appeared, praising God and saying,

"Glory to God in the highest heaven, and on earth peace and good will among those whom he favors!"

After the angels left, the shepherds hurried to Bethlehem. There they found Mary and Joseph and the baby. The shepherds told Mary and Joseph what they had seen and heard, and all were amazed.

Meanwhile, three wise men from the East arrived in Jerusalem, the holy city of Judea. "Where is the baby born to be king of the Jews?" they asked. "We have seen his star in the East and have come to worship him."

King Herod was the ruler of Judea. When he heard that a king of the Jews had been born, he feared that this newborn king would threaten his power. Herod called his priests and scribes together to ask for news about the child.

"The prophets tell us that a leader of the Jews will be born in Bethlehem of Judea," they answered.

Herod sent for the wise men. He thought he could trick them into bringing news about the child, saying that he, too, would like to worship the infant. In truth, Herod planned to kill Jesus.

Again the wise men saw a bright star shining in the East. The star led the men to Bethlehem and shone brightly over the place where Jesus lay. When the wise men saw Mary and the baby, they dropped down to their knees and worshipped the child with joy. Then they opened their treasure chests and presented Jesus with great gifts of gold, frankincense, and myrrh.

The wise men were warned in a dream not to return to King Herod, so they traveled home a different way. When King Herod found out, he was furious. He called for his soldiers and ordered them to go to Bethlehem and kill all the children two years old and under.

Before the soldiers arrived, an angel appeared to Joseph in a dream and told him to go to Egypt for safety. Mary and Joseph fled into the night with their baby. They stayed in Egypt until Herod died, and then they made the long journey back to Nazareth.

Jesus in the Temple

(Luke 2)

very year, Joseph and Mary went to Jerusalem for the festival of Passover. When Jesus was twelve, he made the journey with them.

After the festival ended, Mary, Joseph, and their friends and relatives began the trip back home. When evening came, Mary and Joseph could not find Jesus. They looked for him among their friends and relatives but could not find him anywhere.

Mary and Joseph hurried back to Jerusalem and began to hunt frantically for the child. After searching for three days, they finally found him at the temple. He was sitting among the wise men and religious teachers, listening to them and asking difficult questions. The teachers were amazed at his understanding and his wisdom.

"Child, why have you treated us so?" Mary said. "Your father and I have been searching everywhere for you."

"Why are you searching for me?" Jesus asked. "Did you not know that you could find me in my Father's house?"

Mary and Joseph did not understand Jesus's answer, but Mary kept his words in her heart and treasured them.

After they all returned to Nazareth, Jesus obeyed his parents. He grew up in wisdom and strength and found favor in the eyes of God and his neighbors. Jesus stayed in Nazareth until he was thirty years old.

Jesus in the Wilderness
(Luke 3, Mark 1, Matthew 3–4, John 1)

ighteen years after Jesus was found in the temple, his cousin John the Baptist began preaching in the wilderness of Judea. John preached that all people needed to be baptized and washed clean of their sins. He wore clothes made of camel's hair held together with a wide leather belt. His only food was locusts and wild honey. John baptized scores of people in the river Jordan. When people asked if he was the Messiah, John replied, "After me comes he who is much greater. I am not worthy to stoop down and carry his sandals."

When Jesus was about thirty, he left Galilee and traveled to the river Jordan to be baptized by John. As soon as John saw Jesus, he knew that Jesus was the savior for whom he had been waiting. "Behold the Lamb of God, who takes away the sins of the world!" John cried.

After John baptized Jesus, the heavens opened, and the Holy Spirit descended in the form of a dove, which alighted on Jesus. Then a voice from heaven said, "This is my Son. With you, my beloved, I am well pleased."

After his baptism, Jesus was led by the Holy Spirit into the wilderness. For forty days and forty nights, he ate nothing. When he began to suffer from great hunger, the devil came to tempt him. "If you are the Son of God, order these stones to be turned into bread."

"A person does not live by bread alone," Jesus said, "but by every word that comes from the mouth of God."

Then the devil took Jesus to Jerusalem and led him to the top of the temple roof. "If you are the Son of God, throw yourself down and let the angels rescue you."

"It is wrong to test the power of God," Jesus replied.

Finally, the devil took Jesus to a high mountain, and showed him all the kingdoms of the world and their splendor. "I will give you all of these if you bow down and worship me."

"Away with you, Satan!" Jesus said. "For it is written that we shall worship God and serve him only."

The devil left, and the angels came down and took care of Jesus.

Jesus Chooses His Disciples

(Luke 4–5, Mark 1–2, John 1–2, Matthew 10)

Jesus returned to Nazareth in Galilee and began teaching in the temples. His teachings were called the gospel, which means "good news." Jesus told people that he was the Son of God and that by following him, people could be saved from their sins.

Some people became angry when they heard the words of Jesus. "What right does he have to preach this way?" they asked. "He is only the son of a carpenter." They were so angry they threatened to throw Jesus off a mountain. But he slipped through the crowd and left Nazareth.

As Jesus traveled around Galilee preaching the gospel, his fame grew. Soon large crowds gathered to hear him.

One day as Jesus stood beside the Lake of Galilee, people pressed around him, waiting to hear his words. Jesus climbed into a fishing boat and spoke to the people on the shore.

When he had finished and people began to leave, Jesus told Simon and Andrew, the owners of the boat, to cast their nets into the lake.

"Master, we fished all night and have caught nothing," the two brothers said.

The men lowered their nets. Soon they had such a huge number of fish that their nets began to rip. They called their partners, John and James, for help.

The fishermen were astonished by their great catch. "Fear not," Jesus said to them. "From now on, you shall catch people."

Simon (whom Jesus named Peter), Andrew, John, and James became Jesus's first disciples. The four fishermen left their boats and followed him throughout Galilee as he preached the gospel. They watched as he healed the diseases and afflictions of those who came to him for help. As Jesus's fame spread, people traveled long distances to hear him preach and to be in his presence.

Later Jesus chose eight other disciples from among his followers. Their names were Philip, Matthew, Nathaniel, Thomas, James the son of Alphaeus, Simon the Canaanite, Thaddeus, and Judas Iscariot.

One day there was a wedding in the town of Cana in Galilee. Jesus, his mother, and the disciples were among the guests. During the wedding feast, Mary told Jesus that the wine had run out.

Jesus then ordered the servants to fill six large stone jars with water and take them to the steward.

When the steward tasted the water, he discovered it had been turned into wine. He called out to the bridegroom and said, "People usually serve the best wine first, but you have saved the best wine for last!" When his disciples witnessed this miracle, their belief in Jesus grew even stronger.

The Sermon on the Mount

(Matthew 5–7)

ne day a large crowd had gathered to hear Jesus speak. Jesus climbed to the top of a hill and began to teach and share his great wisdom.

"Blessed are the poor in spirit: for theirs is the kingdom of heaven.
"Blessed are those who mourn: for they shall be comforted.
"Blessed are the meek: for they will inherit the earth.
"Blessed are those who hunger and thirst after righteousness:
*   for they will be filled.*
"Blessed are the merciful: for they will receive mercy.
"Blessed are the pure in heart: for they will see God.
"Blessed are the peacemakers: for they will be called the
*   children of God.*
"Blessed are those who are persecuted for righteousness' sake:
*   for theirs is the kingdom of heaven.*
"Blessed are you when people revile you and persecute you and
*   say all manner of evil against you falsely for my sake.*
"Rejoice, and be exceeding glad, for great is your reward in heaven."

During the Sermon on the Mount, Jesus also said, "Treat others as you wish others to treat you." And he told the crowd to love their enemies as well as their friends and warned that it was only when they could forgive others that God would forgive them.

Jesus also taught his followers a prayer called "The Lord's Prayer":

Our Father who art in heaven,
Hallowed be thy name.
Thy kingdom come,
Thy will be done,
On earth, as it is in heaven.
Give us this day our daily bread.
And forgive us our trespasses,
As we forgive those who trespass against us.
And lead us not into temptation,
But deliver us from evil:
For thine is the kingdom, and the power,
*   and the glory, for ever. Amen.*

Jesus's Great Miracles

(Matthew 14, Luke 9, Mark 6, John 6)

Jesus's fame spread throughout the land, and he sent his disciples out to help spread his message. One day when he and the disciples were all together again, they went to a secluded spot to rest. When people heard that Jesus was nearby, they rushed to be near him. Soon there was a throng of five thousand. Jesus was touched by the needs of the crowd and spent the day teaching and healing the sick.

When evening came, the disciples urged Jesus to send people into the nearby villages to buy food.

"How much food is here?" Jesus asked.

"There are only five loaves of bread and two fishes, belonging to a small boy," the disciples said.

Jesus told everyone to sit down on the grass. Then he blessed the boy's fishes and loaves of bread and gave thanks to God. Then Jesus told his disciples to give food to everyone there. Miraculously, the boy's loaves and fishes multiplied until all five thousand people were fed. There was even enough food left over to fill twelve large baskets.

At the end of the day, Jesus asked the crowds to leave so that he could be alone to pray. He sent his disciples out to sea in a boat; then Jesus went up into the hills. That night strong winds began to blow over the water. As their boat was miles from shore, the disciples were filled with fear. Early in the morning, they looked up and saw Jesus coming toward them. He was walking on the water. The disciples thought it was a ghost, and they were terrified.

"Have heart!" Jesus called to them. "It is I, do not be afraid."

"Lord, if it is you, command me to walk over to you on the water," Peter said.

Peter got out of the boat and began to walk over the water toward Jesus. But when he felt the strong wind, he was afraid and began to sink. "Save me, Lord!" Peter called out. Jesus quickly reached out his hand and caught him.

"O you of little faith," Jesus said, "why did you doubt?"

When Peter and Jesus were safe in the boat, the wind grew calm. Everyone praised and worshipped Jesus. "Truly you are the Son of God," they said.

When Jesus and the disciples reached the shore, crowds were waiting for them. Many had brought their sick to see Jesus. As Jesus walked among them, they reached for the hem of his cloak, and all who touched it were healed.

Some Parables and Teachings

(Luke 10, 15, Matthew 19)

ne day when Jesus was preaching, a lawyer tried to test him. "What must I do to gain eternal life?" he asked.

"What does God's law tell you to do?" Jesus asked.

"The law says you should love the Lord your God with all your heart and soul, and with all your strength, and with all your mind; and you should love your neighbor as yourself," the man answered.

Jesus told the lawyer that his answer was correct and that he should do these things. But the lawyer wanted to test Jesus further. "And who is my neighbor?" he asked.

Jesus then told the parable of a Jewish man traveling from Jerusalem to the city of Jericho. Robbers attacked the man, beat him, and left him for dead.

A priest and another man passed by without stopping.

Then a Samaritan on a donkey came upon the bleeding man and felt pity for him. In those days, Jews and Samaritans did not get along with one another. But the Samaritan bandaged the man's wounds, set him on his donkey, and took him to an inn. All through

the night, the Samaritan cared for the injured man. Before leaving the next morning, the Samaritan gave money to the innkeeper for anything the man might need. "If this is not enough, I will pay you what I owe when I pass by again," he promised.

When Jesus finished his story, he asked the lawyer, "Which of these three men was the man's real neighbor?"

"The one who showed him mercy," the lawyer answered.

"Yes, you are right, and now go and do as the Samaritan did," Jesus said.

One day, Jesus was preaching before a great multitude. The scribes and Pharisees looked at the people with disgust, for there were many poor sinners and outcasts among the crowd.

Seeing their disgust, Jesus explained that the angels felt great joy whenever a sinner repented. Then he told the parable about the prodigal son:

A father divided his property between two sons. The older son stayed at home. The younger son asked for his property and then traveled to a far country, where he wasted his money and lived foolishly. When famine overtook the land, the younger son found himself starving. No one would help him. He was forced to work feeding the pigs in the fields. He himself was so hungry he would have gladly eaten the same food as the pigs. Filled with shame and regret, the young man decided to return home and ask for forgiveness.

His father saw him coming from a long way off and was filled with compassion. Overjoyed, he ran out to embrace his lost son.

"Father, I have sinned against heaven and before you," the son said. "I am no longer worthy to be called your son."

But the happy father ordered his slaves to bring a robe, sandals, and jewelry for the young man. Then he told them to prepare a great feast for his prodigal son. The older brother, who had stayed with his father, watched all of this and said, "Father, I have always served you well, but have never been given a feast."

"Son, you are always with me," said the father, "and all I have is yours. But we must celebrate, for your brother was dead and now is alive. He was lost and now is found."

While Jesus was teaching in a village one day, a group of small children tried to get close to him. The disciples spoke harshly to them and tried to keep the children away, but Jesus stopped them.

"Let the little children come to me," he said, "for the kingdom of God belongs to those who are like children." Then Jesus took the children in his arms, laid his hands on them, and blessed them.

Lazarus Is Raised from the Dead

(John 11)

esus had three close friends who lived in the town of Bethany in Judea. They were Lazarus and his sisters, Mary and Martha.

One day Lazarus got very sick, and Mary and Martha sent a messenger to tell Jesus. Jesus prepared to go to his friends. The disciples warned him that his enemies in Judea might try to harm him. "Our friend Lazarus has fallen asleep," Jesus said. "I am going there to awaken him."

But by the time Jesus arrived, Lazarus had died and had been lying in his tomb for four days. Martha met Jesus along the way. "Lord, if you had been here, my brother would not have died!" she cried.

Jesus was greatly disturbed. "Your brother will rise again," Jesus promised. "I am the resurrection and the life. Even though they die, those who believe in me, yet shall they live."

Martha, Mary, and their friends led Jesus to the cave where Lazarus was buried. After they rolled back the stone that covered the entrance, Jesus lifted his eyes and prayed to his Father. Then he called out, "Lazarus, come forth!"

To everyone's amazement, Lazarus rose from the dead and came out from the cave with his face, hands, and feet still bound in strips of burial cloth.

"Unbind him, and let him go," Jesus said.

After this miracle, Jesus's fame became so great that the chief priests and scribes met in a council. "What are we going to do?" they asked fearfully. "If we do nothing, everyone will believe what he says is true." And from then on, Jesus's enemies plotted to arrest Jesus and have him put to death.

Jesus's Entry into Jerusalem
(Matthew 21, 26, Mark 11, Luke 19–20, John 2, 12)

When the festival of Passover drew near, crowds flocked into Jerusalem for the celebration. Many were also waiting excitedly for Jesus to arrive. Drawing near the city, Jesus asked two disciples to find him a donkey to ride.

As Jesus rode the donkey into Jerusalem, people gathered along the roadside, cheering and waving. Many threw their cloaks on the pavement to line his way. And others waved palm branches, shouting, "Hosanna! Blessed is the King who comes in the name of the Lord! Peace in heaven and glory in the highest!"

When the Pharisees saw the people greeting Jesus, they went to him and asked him to stop them. "If I make them stop, all the stones will weep," Jesus said.

Jesus passed through the great city gate and made his way to the temple of Jerusalem. When he arrived, he found its courtyard teeming with money changers and vendors selling pigeons, sheep, and oxen.

Filled with fury, Jesus overthrew the tables and scattered the money. "My Father's house is a house of prayer," he said. "But you have turned it into a den of robbers!"

Jesus's enemies were afraid to arrest him in front of the crowd. But soon a man came to them and offered to betray Jesus. The man was Judas, one of Jesus's twelve disciples. In exchange for thirty pieces of silver, Judas promised to deliver Jesus to them.

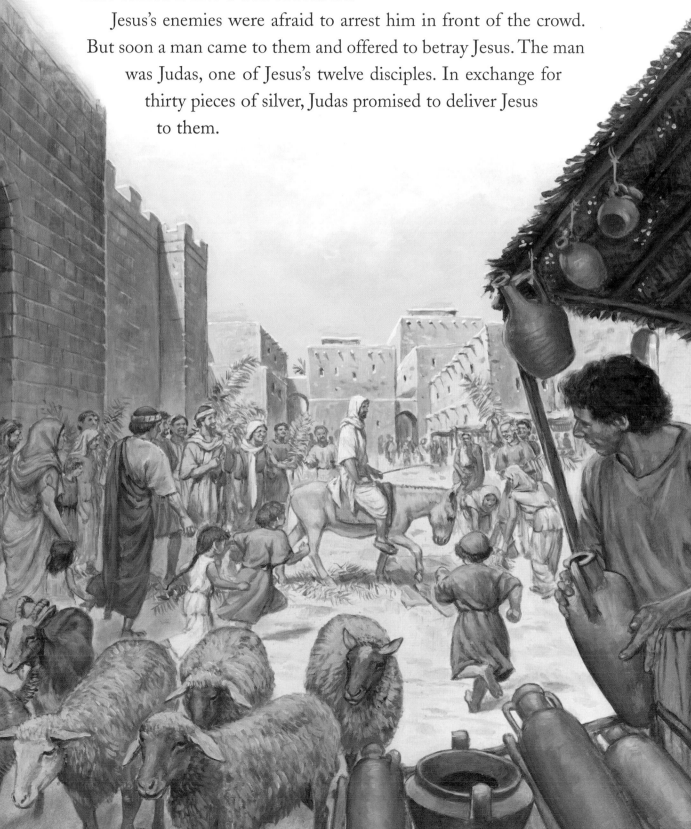

The Last Supper

(Matthew 26, Mark 14, Luke 22, John 13)

On the night of the Passover feast, Jesus and his disciples gathered in an upper room of a house. When they were seated at the table, Jesus got water and linen cloth and washed their feet. As he was doing this, Simon Peter asked, "Lord, why are you washing my feet?"

"You do not understand what I am doing now," Jesus answered. "But you will understand later."

Then Jesus blessed the bread, gave thanks, and broke it, giving a piece to each of them and saying, "Take, eat, for this is my body." After his disciples ate the bread, Jesus blessed the wine, and passed it around to them. "Drink this," he said, "for this is my blood, which is shed for you."

As they were sharing the Passover meal, Jesus told his disciples that soon one of them would betray him.

The disciples looked sorrowfully at Jesus. "Is it I?" "Is it I?" they asked, but Jesus did not answer.

"Lord, who is he?" Peter whispered.

"The one to whom I now give this bread," Jesus told Peter, and he handed a piece of bread to Judas. "What you must do, do quickly," Jesus said. Judas took the bread and hurried out to betray Jesus to his enemies.

Jesus told his disciples that he was soon going to leave them. "Where I am going you cannot come," he said.

"Lord, where will you go?" asked Peter.

"Where I am going you cannot follow," said Jesus.

"But why?" Peter asked. "I would lay down my life for you."

"Will you lay down your life for me, Peter?" Jesus asked his dearest disciple. "Very truly, I tell you, before the rooster crows, you will deny three times that you ever knew me."

The apostles sang a hymn with Jesus and followed him out of the upper room into the night, up to the Mount of Olives.

Jesus in the Garden
(Matthew 26, Mark 14, Luke 22, John 18)

Jesus took Peter, John, and James with him to a garden called Gethsemane on the Mount of Olives. He turned to them and said, "My soul is filled with sorrow, and I am greatly grieved. Sit here and stay awake while I pray."

Jesus walked a stone's throw away. Then he lay down with his face to the ground. He began to pray, "Father, all things are possible to you. Let this cup pass from me. And let your will be done, not mine."

Three times Jesus found his disciples had fallen asleep, and three times he woke them. The third time he said, "Are you still sleeping? The hour has come when the Son of Man is betrayed into the hands of sinners."

As Jesus finished speaking, Judas and a band of soldiers entered the garden, carrying lanterns, swords, and clubs. Judas had told them to arrest the man whom he kissed.

"Greetings, Teacher," Judas said, and kissed Jesus.

The soldiers seized Jesus. As they led him away, all the disciples fled except Peter, who followed at a distance.

The soldiers took Jesus to the house of the high priest. There they blindfolded him and began beating and mocking him.

Out in the courtyard, Peter waited with the guards warming themselves by the fire. A servant girl pointed at him.

"You were with Jesus," she said.

Peter was terrified. "I don't know what you are talking about," he declared. Then another maid pointed at him and said, "This is the man who was with Jesus of Nazareth." Again Peter denied that it was true.

When a soldier accused Peter of knowing Jesus, Peter turned angrily and said, "Have I not already told you? I do not know this man!"

At that moment, the rooster crowed. Peter remembered Jesus's words: *Before the rooster crows, you will deny three times that you ever knew me.*

Peter wept with shame and ran from the courtyard.

Jesus Goes Before Pilate

(Matthew 27, Mark 15, Luke 23, John 18–19)

orning came, and Jesus's captors bound him and dragged him before Pilate, the governor from Rome. When Pilate asked him questions, Jesus stood before him and answered simply and quietly, neither arguing nor agreeing. "I can find no reason to accuse this man," Pilate finally said. But Jesus's enemies insisted that Jesus had stirred up crowds from Galilee to Judea.

Now it was a custom during the Passover festival for Pilate to release one prisoner.

Pilate turned to the crowd and asked, "What do you wish me to do, release Barabbas or this man, Jesus? What do you wish me to do with Jesus?"

"Crucify him! Crucify him!" the crowd yelled.

"Why? What crime has he committed?" Pilate asked.

But they shouted all the more, "Let him be crucified!"

Pilate asked for a bowl of water and washed his hands. "I am innocent of this man's blood," he declared. After he released Barabbas, Pilate handed Jesus over to the mob.

The soldiers put a scarlet robe on Jesus and twisted some thorns into a crown and placed it on his head. Then they knelt in front of him, jeering, "Hail, King of the Jews!" And they spat on him and beat him until finally they led Jesus away to be crucified.

The Crucifixion

(Matthew 27, Mark 15, Luke 23, John 19)

esus was taken to a place called Golgotha, which means "Place of the Skull." Over Jesus's head they placed a sign that read "This is Jesus, King of the Jews." The crowd jeered and called out, "If you are King of the Jews, why don't you come down from the cross and save yourself?" Soldiers began dividing up Jesus's clothes and throwing lots to see who would get them. As he was suffering and near death, Jesus prayed: *"Father, forgive them, for they do not know what they do."*

Watching from a distance were Jesus's mother, Mary, and his friend Mary Magdalene. They were filled with sorrow as they saw Jesus's suffering on the cross.

At noon, darkness descended over the earth. It lasted until three o'clock. At that hour, Jesus cried out, "My God, my God, why have you forsaken me?"

The soldiers mocked him, and a man in the crowd gave Jesus vinegar on a sponge to moisten his lips.

Then Jesus cried out in a loud voice, "Father, into your hands I commend my spirit!"

As he breathed his last breath, he said, "It is finished."

Suddenly the earth shook and rocks broke apart. A Roman soldier guarding Jesus looked on in awe. "Truly this man was the Son of God," he said.

The Resurrection

(Matthew 28, Mark 16, Luke 24, John 20)

Two days later, Mary Magdalene came to the tomb early in the morning with spices to anoint the body of Jesus. It was still dark, but to her amazement, she could see that the stone in front of the tomb had been rolled back. She ran quickly to tell Peter and John.

"They have taken our Lord from the tomb, and I do not know where they have laid him!" Mary cried.

The two disciples ran back to the tomb with her. They found the burial linen but not the body of Jesus. Peter and John did not understand what had happened. They returned home, but Mary remained at the tomb weeping.

While she was grieving, Mary saw two angels sitting where the body of Jesus had been. They asked her why she was crying.

"Because they have taken away my Lord," Mary said, "and I do not know where they have laid him."

As Mary said this, she turned and saw a man standing nearby who she thought was the gardener.

"Mary," the man said simply.

Suddenly Mary knew the man was Jesus. "Teacher!" she cried.

"Now go to my disciples," Jesus told her, "and tell them you have seen me and that soon I will go to my Father, who is also your Father, and to my God, who is your God."

Mary ran to the disciples and told them that she had seen Jesus, and shared all the words he had spoken to her.

The Ascension

(Luke 24, Mark 16, Matthew 28, John 20)

The eleven grieving apostles gathered in Jerusalem. Suddenly Jesus appeared before them. The men thought they were seeing a ghost and were confused and afraid.

Jesus tried to calm their fears. "Peace be with you. Why are you troubled? Why do so many questions arise in your hearts? See my hands and my feet," he said. "A ghost does not have flesh and bones as I have.

"Now go into all the world," Jesus said, "and proclaim the good news to all of creation. Preach a message of repentance and forgiveness both far and wide. Teach people to observe all the things I have shared with you, and remember that I am with you always, even unto the end of the world."

Jesus led the apostles as far as Bethany; then he lifted up his hands and blessed them. And while he was blessing them, he was carried up into heaven by God.

Filled with great joy, the apostles returned to Jerusalem. Soon they would go out into the world to tell the story of Jesus Christ.